"All right, everybo
"This is our best opp

Laika had just ans
Ricardo felt, the cre
sat at his station witl
brain to the ship's computer. Chief Engineer Georgie
LaForgery had rigged up this connection. It made Dacron a barking interface between Laika and the computer's 20th-century-Russian memory banks.

Laika woofed at them from the Viewscreen. Dacron's eyeballs shifted from side to side. "Arf!" Dacron responded.

"Arf?" answered Laika, cocking her head at him.

"Arf! Arf!" said Dacron . . .

STAR WRECK 7
Space, The Fido Frontier
A PARODY

St. Martin's Paperbacks Titles by Leah Rewolinski

STAR WRECK: THE GENERATION GAP
STAR WRECK 2: THE ATTACK OF THE JARGONITES
STAR WRECK 3: TIME WARPED
STAR WRECK 4: LIVE LONG AND PROFIT
STAR WRECK 5: THE UNDISCOVERED NURSING HOME
STAR WRECK 6: GEEK SPACE NINE
STAR WRECK 7: SPACE, THE FIDO FRONTIER

STAR WRECK 7

SPACE, THE FIDO FRONTIER

A creative collection
of cosmic canine cut-ups

by

LEAH REWOLINSKI
ILLUSTRATIONS BY
HARRY TRUMBORE

A 2M COMMUNICATIONS LTD. PRODUCTION

ST. MARTIN'S PAPERBACKS

Star Wreck is an unauthorized parody of the *Star Trek* television and motion picture series, the *Star Trek: The Next Generation* television series, and the *Star Trek: Deep Space Nine* television series. None of the individuals or companies associated with these series or with any merchandise based upon these series, has in any way sponsored, approved, endorsed or authorized this book.

Published by arrangement with the author

STAR WRECK 7: SPACE, THE FIDO FRONTIER

ISBN: 0-312-95362-3

Printed in the United States of America

St. Martin's Paperbacks edition / December 1994

10 9 8 7 6 5 4 3 2 1

To the best husband in the universe and God's gift to women of all species, I pledge my eternal gratitude for getting me interested in "Star Trek."

P.S. Thanks for helping out my busy schedule by writing this dedication for me.

GOOD LUCKSKI, LITTLE SOCIALIST DOG

Acknowledgments

These have been the voyages of the starship *Endocrine.* As I cruise onward looking for novel predicaments to get into, many thanks to all whose encouragement and enthusiam for the journey have enabled me to "make it so"—including John Rounds of St. Martin's Press, whose expertise has touched every volume of *Star Wreck.*

Special thanks to Harry Trumbore, illustrator extraordinaire, whose pictures are worth a thousand words.

And let's not forget Laika, the original space explorer, who gave her all for The Fido Frontier.

Contents

1

The Bark Heard 'Round the World

"CAPTAIN'S LOG, Stardate 36-point-24-point-36. My Bridge crewmembers and I have been summoned from our beds by an urgent message from Starfreak Command insisting on an immediate phone meeting."

Capt. Jean-Lucy Ricardo stifled a yawn, surveying the Bridge of the USS *Endocrine* as he finished his audio log entry.

"We await the connection of our Viewscreen with one at Starfreak Headquarters in Milwaukee."

The command center of the starship was subdued during night watch. The beeping of computers and the chatter of crewmembers were stilled at this hour, allowing subtle night noises to creep through: softly chirping crickets; a sump pump clicking on, whirring smoothly, then clicking off again; the water softener swishing through its regeneration cycle.

Night lights in the corners of the room cast a glow over the dimmed panels of consoles and science stations. The furnace blower kicked in, its *whoosh* of musty warmth especially welcome now that the thermostat had been set to "low" for several hours.

To Ricardo's right, Cmdr. Wilson Piker snored raggedly. Piker hadn't bothered to grease his hair into submission before stumbling to the Bridge, so his bangs fell fetchingly over his forehead.

On Ricardo's left, the empathic Counselor Deanna "Dee" Troit slumped in her chair, her head lolling around on the backrest. As the ship rocked slightly over some turbulence, a gentle swaying beneath her tunic hinted that in her hurry to get to the Bridge, Troit had forgotten to put on a strategic piece of lingerie. For once, she didn't seem to be "sensing something," except perhaps the need to crawl back into bed.

Lt. Cmdr. Dacron rose from his Oops console in the forward section and lurched toward the center of the Bridge. The android wore an unusually bleary expression, and Capt. Ricardo realized that Dacron was having another one of his waking dreams—probably that slasher dream again, for he seemed about to attack Counselor Troit with a Ginzu knife.

"Dacron!" Ricardo called. Dacron came to his senses and slinked back to his seat.

Lt. Wart stood at his Tactical station on the platform in back of Ricardo. The Kringle had left his quarters without bothering to tie back his ponytail, and the thick mane of hair cascading down his shoulders made him look like the bulkiest Breck Girl of all time.

Wart checked his console panel and announced, "Captain, we are being hailed by Starfreak Command."

"Onscreen," sighed Ricardo.

As the Starfreak logo appeared on the Viewscreen, a bone-chilling howl blasted from the speakers.

"Ooooooooooooooowwwwooooowwooo!"

Capt. Ricardo bolted back in his chair. Counselor Troit jerked awake, wide-eyed with panic. Dacron, zapped into a positronic overload, wet his pants.

Wart reflexively vaulted over the rail to the center of the Bridge and took a martial arts stance, then backed off sheepishly as he realized that the threat was, so far, nonexistent.

On the Viewscreen, the Starfreak Command logo was replaced by the image of an admiral wearing a cardigan sweater over her Starfreak tunic. Most of her silvery hair was tied back in a bun, though many strands had escaped, straggling around her face.

The staff recognized her as Admiral Mia Culpa. Her picture had appeared with an article about her 75th service anniversary in the previous issue of Starfreak Command's newsletter, *Command-Dope*.

"How did you like *that*, Jean-Lucy?!" Admiral Culpa inquired cheerily.

"I'm afraid . . ." Capt. Ricardo gasped, "it was . . . a bit . . . much . . . for me, Admiral."

"Oh, dear," said Admiral Culpa, pressing a hand to her lips. "I've startled you, haven't I? Oh, I'm so sorry."

"No harm done, Admiral," Capt. Ricardo said with the El Plastico grin he often trotted out for admiral encounters.

"But I've scared the living daylights out of you." Admiral Culpa plucked at the sleeve of her sweater. "What a dreadful blunder. I just wanted to get your attention and make sure everyone was awake, that's all. Ever since I started making my long-distance Viewscreen calls after eleven o'clock to get the lower rate, people tend to fall asleep on me."

"Admiral, what *was* that noise?" Piker wanted to know.

Admiral Culpa answered with another question. "Captain Ricardo . . . Commander Piker . . . Does the name Laika mean anything to you?"

The two of them racked their brains, eager to look good to the admiral, but it was obvious that neither of them knew the answer. Finally Capt. Ricardo muttered, "Dacron, help us out here."

Dacron piped up, "Laika was a dog of the twentieth century who was the first living creature to enter space and experience weightlessness. She rode aboard a spacecraft launched by the Union of Soviet Socialist Republics. Logic would suggest that the noise we just heard was a recording of Laika's howl."

"That's correct, Lieutenant," Admiral Culpa said. "Thank you. So, you see—"

"The mission began on November third, 1957," Dacron went on. "Laika herself was of unknown pedigree and weighed 11 pounds."

"Very good, Lieutenant," Culpa said. "Now—"

"Unfortunately," Dacron interrupted again, "the spacecraft was launched with no plans to return Laika to Earth. She is believed to have perished when her seven-day supply of oxygen ran out. The Humane Society of the Milky Way is still investigating the incident."

"That will be *all*, Lieutenant," Culpa directed.

Dacron didn't seem to notice the edge in Culpa's tone. "Perhaps we could pinpoint Laika's pedigree by combing the databanks for breeds with a typical adult weight of 11 pounds," he mused, "and cross-referencing it with Universal Kennel Club records of breeds in existence at that time . . ."

"Number One." Ricardo made a finger-across-the-throat gesture to indicate that Piker should help Dacron put a lid on it.

Piker sneaked up on Dacron from the back and pressed the android's "off" switch, but nothing happened. He jiggled the switch back and forth without success.

"The mission raises other intriguing questions," Dacron went on. "For instance, was Laika's waste simply jettisoned from the capsule and left to drift in space? Or had the Soviets secretly developed a prototype robotic arm to function as a pooper scooper?"

Frustrated by the inoperable "off" switch, Piker clamped a hand over Dacron's mouth. Dacron's babbling continued, somewhat muffled.

Ricardo smiled at the Viewscreen. "You were saying, Admiral?" he asked, as if everything were normal.

Admiral Culpa raised her voice to make herself heard

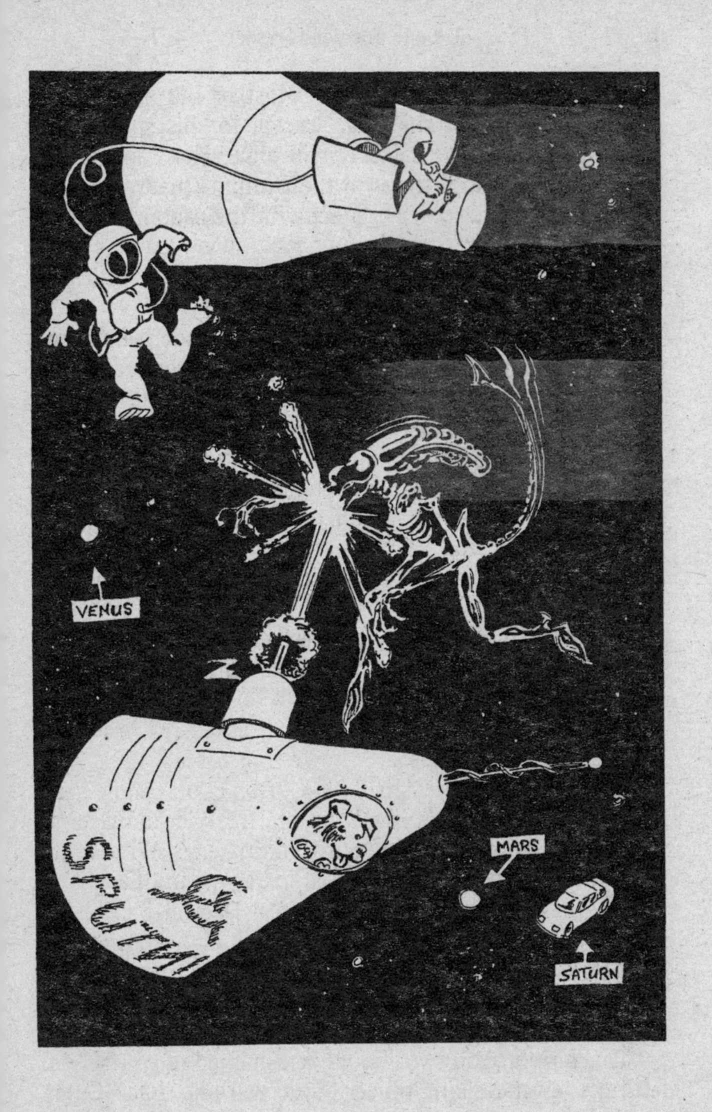

"The mission raises other intriguing questions."

over Dacron's muffled chatter. "Most of the lieutenant's report is accurate," she said, "except for his speculation about Laika's death. Laika is still alive. Her capsule has been spotted several times in the Gummi Quadrant. Most recently, she made voice contact with the captain of a Macaronian freighter."

"But if she was launched several centuries ago," Ricardo asked, "how can she be alive today?"

"Periodic reports have hinted that she underwent some sort of genetic transformation," Culpa replied. "Her capsule passed through the wormhole into the Gummi Quadrant after drifting off course about six days into her twentieth-century mission. The transition through the wormhole slowed Laika's metabolism tremendously. For her, each people-year is only worth about one one-hundredth of a dog year. As for her oxygen supply, we suspect that Ferengi traders sold her some air-recycling technology."

"Admiral, this is all very interesting," Ricardo said in a tone that couldn't help hinting he thought it was anything but. "Can you tell me what it has to do with Starfreak?"

"You don't have any idea?" Culpa asked. Ricardo and Piker shook their heads.

Culpa continued in a shrill tone, "Don't you people keep up with current events involving Starfreak Headquarters? Come now, fellows. Put on your thinking caps. Why would Starfreak Command be interested in recovering Laika?"

The question hung in the air until Dacron bit Piker's finger, forcing Piker to drop his hand long enough for Dacron to blurt out: "Because of the Classic Creatures exhibition!" Piker clamped a hand over Dacron's face again with a little extra force.

"That's right. You two should be ashamed of yourselves, letting a lower-ranking officer outdo you like that," Culpa scolded. "As the lieutenant guessed, we want Laika as a permanent addition to the Classic Creatures exhibition at

"It was popular from the day it opened."

the Milwaukee Public Museum. If you had even a passing knowledge of civic events, you'd have heard of it.

"It was popular from the day it opened, exhibiting the preserved bodies of Cheetah—Tarzan's chimpanzee—and Flipper the dolphin. And now that we've constructed the Starfreak Space Animals Wing of the museum, which includes an exhibit featuring Ripley's cat, attendance has tripled."

"So you must be counting on Laika to draw attention because she's space-related, too," Ricardo said.

Admiral Culpa nodded. "*And*, she's alive. Laika will be a tremendous hit. Starfreak receives a portion of each paid admission. We anticipate a huge increase in revenue from the wing once Laika is installed in her new living quarters, so we are offering a generous finder's fee if your crew brings her back alive." Culpa primly smoothed her sweater, adding, "We're paying in Starfreak Reserve Notes, not gold-pressed laudanum, so there won't be any problem with fluctuating exchange rates."

"We'll get right on it, Admiral," Ricardo said, anticipating the end of the call.

"Oh, by the way, there's one more little thing, Captain," Admiral Culpa added. "This will be your last mission. Once you finish it, Starfreak plans to put your crew on furlough."

"What?" Ricardo asked in an astonished whisper. Everyone else on the Bridge stared in shock. Dacron stopped chattering.

Ricardo protested weakly, "But we've done so well on all our missions lately. We've gotten commendations, citations, bonuses . . ."

"I can't quibble with that," Culpa agreed. "You've done a dandy job. The trouble is, you've all got so much seniority that Starfreak can't afford to keep your crew on active duty anymore. But you needn't worry. The finder's fee we're offering for Laika should supplement your retirement annuities—enough to keep all of you out of the poorhouse, I should think.

"Our space missions will continue, of course, but from now on they'll be conducted by newcomers on the USS *V-Ger*. We've hired them at a pittance of your salaries.

"Well, that's it for now," Culpa concluded brightly. "Time to settle down with my quilt and an Agatha Crispie novel. Goodnight, all." She signed off the Viewscreen.

"That bloody hen," Ricardo growled.

"Captain," said Counselor Troit, "I sense that our officers are unhappy over the news that this is our last assignment."

"You don't say," Ricardo muttered.

Troit remarked cheerfully to the others on the Bridge, "But look at it this way: for once we're not trying to outdo Captain Smirk's crewmembers on the same mission. Since they've voluntarily disbanded, we can just go about our business without having them breathing down our necks."

Capt. Ricardo was not about to be jollied out of his bad mood so easily. Glaring at Troit, he announced, "There you have it, ladies and gentlemen: today's words of wisdom from Counselor Pollyanna Troit."

Ricardo settled into his chair and ordered, "Ensign, set course for the wormhole to the Gummi Quadrant. Warped seven. Engage." The ship took off, leaving behind a trail of blue warped-drive exhaust particles at a rate just barely under EPA maximum-emission standards.

As the conversation between Adm. Culpa and Capt. Ricardo ended, a certain Vulture turned down the volume of the ham radio he was using to monitor the transmission from afar. Starfreak's interest in locating Laika in the Gummi Quadrant was such very, very good news that, for a moment, the eavesdropper was in danger of smiling. Then Mr. Smock regained control and considered the logical course of action.

Here, finally, was the break he'd awaited. For months

he'd been at loose ends as Capt. James T. Smirk savored the delights of the Planet of the Amazon Women. There was little for Smock to do but categorize the planet's indigenous rock samples and recalibrate the computers of their ship, parked here in a vacant lot. He'd bided his time, knowing from experience that eventually Smirk would want to move on.

At last, a few days ago, Capt. Smirk began showing the inevitable signs of boredom and restlessness. He mused that variety was the spice of life. He asked Smock to retrieve some databank information on the Planet of the Lilliputian Ladies. He even speculated about "getting the guys together for one more gig."

That gig, Mr. Smock reasoned, had just revealed itself in the form of Starfreak's interest in Laika. It didn't matter that the mission officially belonged to Smirk's chief rival, Capt. Ricardo. In fact, that would only heighten Smirk's interest in the chase.

Even so, Smock knew that it wasn't enough just to mention the idea to his captain; he had to put the right spin on it, too, because Smirk was only mildly dissatisfied with the Planet of the Amazon Women. At this stage, Smirk was like a piece of popcorn wedged between two molars—he could be dislodged, but only with finesse.

The solution sprang to Smock's mind the next morning when he spotted Capt. Smirk bathing in the pond beneath the waterfall. Four of the Amazon Women had carried Smirk there on a litter for his morning dip. Smirk's obvious fondness for these large and lovely companions inspired Smock with a way to sell the sizzle of the new mission. He explained the idea as Smirk bathed.

"The Gummi Quadrant, hmmm?" Smirk repeated, lathering up with his soap-on-a-rope. "Countless alien women still to be discovered and conquered there, you say?"

As was customary, the Amazon Women were kneeling, eyes averted, at the edge of the pond next to Smirk's terrycloth robe. Two of them began to giggle. Mr. Smock could discern no reason for their high spirits, but Capt. Smirk was right on their wavelength.

"Uh-uh, ladies," Smirk said, fondly wagging his index finger at them. "No *peek*-ing." This prompted a chorus of giggles from all four.

Mr. Smock steered the conversation back to business. "The Gummi Quadrant is largely unexplored," he told Smirk. "There is no telling what exotic life forms we might encounter."

Smirk scrubbed his back with a loofah sponge. "Sounds promising," he acknowledged. "And what's this business about a dog?"

As Smock recounted details of the reward being offered for capturing Laika, Smirk began shampooing his hair, nodding thoughtfully. When Smock finished his spiel, Smirk waded over to the thundering waterfall to rinse off, singing "Lucy in the Sky with Diamonds" at the top of his lungs.

By the time he stepped out onto the bank, Smirk had made up his mind. "Well, Smock, what are you waiting for?" he asked. "Let's round up the crew, shall we?" Wrapped in his robe, he plopped down onto the litter and ordered, "Ladies, start your engines."

For the first stop on their crew-roundup drive, Capt. Smirk and Mr. Smock steered their *Endocrine* into orbit of Earth and took a shuttle down to a country club called I'm A Doctor Except on Thursdays. They knew they would find Dr. Lynyrd McCaw there, for he was the club's owner and manager.

Sure enough, they spotted McCaw the minute they entered the pro shop of the clubhouse. Their former crewmate and chief medical officer seemed to be everywhere at once: announcing tee times over the p.a. system with the authoritative tone he'd formerly used to boss around nurses; plucking golf balls out of the discount jar with his delicate surgeon's touch; and diagnosing the broken shaft of a customer's #3 wood: "Compound fracture. Inoperable. Lucky for you, we have drivers on sale this month."

The phone rang, and McCaw answered: "Mercy Hospital." His face registered annoyance at the caller's inquiry. "Yes, Doctor Haramkrishnatoejama signed in here this morning, but he can't be reached . . . . You think you're the only person with an emergency? He's handling a very touchy case right now . . . . There's no way of knowing how long it will take . . . . All right, hold on a second." McCaw stabbed the "hold" button and hollered at a waitress in the snack bar: "Sally, how far along is Rahjid's foursome?"

Glancing out the window, the waitress reported, "They're just teeing off at the back nine."

McCaw retrieved his caller. "He's in surgery," McCaw barked. "It'll be at least two hours." He slammed down the receiver.

The irritation that had twisted McCaw's features lifted immediately when he spotted Capt. Smirk and Mr. Smock. "Well, I'll be a monkey's hernia," he said with a grin. "Look what just warped in here."

"Moans," Capt. Smirk called heartily. "How have you been, you old rascal?"

McCaw insisted that they visit the snack bar for a drink on the house. Mr. Smock, who was usually not too keen on socializing, came along willingly just to get away from the pro shop; the displays of plaid sports slacks were making him nauseous.

The three officers ordered iced tea and took a table. Smirk got right to the point, asking McCaw to join them in the pursuit of Laika.

McCaw scrunched up his face as he considered the idea. "I had been thinking about taking a vacation," he allowed, "but lately things are going pretty smoothly around here, so I thought I'd just kick back and enjoy them for a—"

BAM! The screen door leading to the first tee slammed inward on the wall. The deafening roar of an engine filled

BAM! The screen door leading to the first tee slammed inward.

the room as a mower rattled toward them, scenting the air with gasoline and dropping shavings of bentgrass on the carpet. Riding the mower toward Dr. McCaw was Smirk's former chief engineer, Montgomery Ward Snot.

He looked mightily annoyed until he spotted Smirk and Smock. Then he switched off the engine and wiped his hands on his overalls, lumbering toward them with a big smile.

"Holy mother o' pearl," he cried. "Do my eyes deceive me, or is it really you, Cap'n? And Misterrr Smock!" He gave them each a mighty bear hug, leaving grass stains on their uniforms. "This calls for a round o' drinks on you, don't ya think?"

"Snot," Dr. McCaw said drily, "would you mind telling me why you drove that mower in here?"

"Aacchh," said Snot, annoyance shadowing his face once again. "Th' confounded machine is ready for the scrrrrap heap. I thought you should hear it for y'self—the engine is pingin' and gaspin' somethin' terrible. I can't get a decent cut w' those old blades, either. Look a' these!" He scooped up a handful of tiny grass clippings from the carpet and dumped them on the table.

McCaw stared. "What about them?"

Snot *tsk-tsked* indignantly. "Can't ye see it, mon? They're uneven! An' that means the fairways are uneven, too. The customers can't get a decent drive on uneven fairways."

The pile of clippings ignited McCaw's grass allergy. His eyes watered. "Snotty, when did you start caring about the customers?" he demanded. He held a finger to his nose, trying to stifle a sneeze. "This is just a bad excuse for getting me to kick in for another new mower. But I . . . I . . . ah . . . ah . . . ah*choo*!" The grass clippings fluttered onto the iced tea glasses like a shower of green snowflakes.

Glaring first at Snot and then at his mower, which was leaking oil on the carpet, McCaw shook his head. He turned to Smirk: "So all we'd have to do on this mission is find a dog and bring her home?"

"That's it," Smirk affirmed.

"Let's do it," McCaw announced. "Snot, call up that high school kid who cuts the grass on Sundays. Ask him to fill in for you for a few weeks. We're going on a mission."

"Hot diggity dog!" Snot replied with relish, glad to catch up on the old routine and get his buns in gear again.

Within a few days, Smirk and Smock had gathered together all but one of their fellow *Endocrine*-ers.

Pavlov Checkout, they discovered, was keeping a full schedule. When he wasn't working at the drive-up window of McTofuburger, he was directing one of his twenty Flub Scout troops—the next best thing, he figured, to his ever-elusive goal of earning command rank in Starfreak.

Communications Officer Yoohoo was busy, too, selling Murray Kay beauty products from the trunk of her pink Cadillac. Capt. Smirk burst in on one of her home demonstration parties, setting the ladies all a-twitter.

Neither Checkout nor Yoohoo really wanted to put their brilliant careers on hold for another mission in space. However, since their main incomes came from Starfreak pensions, and since Smirk signed their pension checks each month, they didn't have much choice but to join Smirk's merry band.

The final crewmember, Hikup Zulu, was unaware that his six former shipmates were tracking him down. For Zulu, today promised to be just another tranquil, contemplative, utterly boring day.

Zulu's new home, a monastery called the Yin/Yang Lamma Lamma Ding Dong Retreat, was tucked so far into the hills that only the most determined visitors ever came to the door. And since the rules of the order encompassed poverty, chastity, and eating a bulb of garlic daily, few visitors hung around for very long, either.

A few minutes before his crewmates' arrival, Zulu was

deeply immersed in a solitary meditation corresponding to the monastery's current fun event: The Silence of a Hundred Days. Talking was not allowed for any reason, even in emergencies. Zulu, one of the novices in the order, had been severely reprimanded in the first week of The Silence for whispering "Please pass the Listerine."

That was 96 days ago. Ever since then, Zulu had adhered to the rules. His initial doubts about his new vocation began lifting as the end of The Silence neared. Zulu knew that if he could refrain from speaking till the very last day, he would achieve an inner peace that would make it all worthwhile. Already the enforced silence and heavy-duty meditation had quieted the usual noises in his head; it had been weeks since he'd been haunted by the theme from "Jeopardy."

A gong sounded. Zulu rose and joined the others in the corridor who were shuffling to the midday group meditation. Today it was Zulu's turn to sit meditating in front of the group, demonstrating peace and utter calm, sending out inspiring vibrations to his brothers in the Order of the Glass Noodle.

Zulu knelt at the spot of honor in front of the assembly. The monk in charge of the sound system cued up a CD, "Sound of One Hand Clapping." Everyone closed their eyes and hunkered down deep inside their souls.

They were over an hour into a richly satisfying group grok when Zulu sensed a discordant element in the room. He'd learned to ignore this; it usually meant that someone was longing for former worldly pleasures like cable TV or Good & Plenty candy. When the meditator overcame the urge, Zulu had learned, the vibe would subside.

Yet this time the dissonance was not fading on its own. Disturbed, Zulu opened his eyes. And there at the back of the room was Capt. Smirk, greeting him with a smile and a thumbs-up gesture.

"Captain Smirk!" blurted out the astonished Zulu.

His exclamation threw a shock wave through the room.

Eyelids flew open. Sharply indrawn breath rustled like the wind. "You spoke!" one of the other novices said.

"So did you!" said another.

"Silence, you two!" an elderly monk ordered. Then he clamped a hand over his mouth in horror.

Astonishment loosened the tongues of others, despite their best intentions. "Quiet!" "You are breaking The Silence!" "You started it!" "Did not!" "Did too!" "Stop it, all of you!"

Their finely honed group concentration sized up the situation an instant later, and dagger-like stares pinpointed Smirk and Zulu as the perpetrators. Smirk and Zulu bolted through the door and charged down the stone-paved corridor.

The mob of enraged monks and novices followed. Their shouts joined in a tremendous uproar; since The Silence had been breached anyway, they figured *What the heck?*

"Sorry about this," Smirk panted. "I didn't mean to get you in trouble."

"Oh, well," Zulu replied, his vocal cords too rusty to express his dismay. He concentrated on keeping a few steps ahead of the surging crowd and tried not to think of the few possessions he was leaving behind: his diary, a Slinky toy, and two tubes of Brylcreem.

A string of prayer beads flung by one of the monks whistled past, narrowly missing Zulu's skull and reminding him that they weren't yet out of the woods. Smirk and Zulu sprinted across the front lawn toward Smirk's *Endocrine*, which floated on its pontoons in the middle of the monastery's lily pond. "Smock! Smock! Start the engine!" Capt. Smirk cried.

Smock sat on the starboard pontoon lazily dipping his fishing pole into the water. Just as Smirk and Zulu appeared, a fish nibbled on Smock's line. A lesser man might have been torn between catching the fish and saving his boss from the approaching mob, but Smock made a more logical move: he simply fastened the pole to a strut on the

The mob of enraged monks and novices followed.

ship, keeping the fish on line while he climbed into the ship and gunned the engine to life. Smirk and Zulu jumped into the water and swam toward the *Endocrine*. As Smock began the takeoff, they lifted themselves onto the pontoon just in time, stepping across it like wing-walkers on a stunt plane.

Zulu, mindful of the monastery's catch-and-release policy, removed the hook from the fish's mouth and let the creature drop back into the pond. It swam away, looking far more peaceful than the monks standing on the shore, shaking their fists and howling as the ship disappeared into space.

2

Over the River and Through the Wormhole

"THIS IS THE THIRD time we've passed that asteroid with the historical marker on it," Counselor Troit observed. "We must be going in circles." Capt. Ricardo stared at the ceiling of the Bridge, refusing to acknowledge her remark.

Ricardo's crew was already a half-day's flight into the Gummi Quadrant. They'd entered the wormhole without stopping at Geek Space Nine to refuel or to pick up maps because Ricardo was leery of running into the space station's commander, Bungeeman Crisco.

Ricardo had enjoyed a temporary truce with Crisco for a while after the crew's last mission, when Dacron helped lift the dullimia plague on the station. However, dullimia soon resettled over the GS-Niners. When Crisco's gratitude faded, he resumed his grudge over Ricardo's role in the death of his wife during the Bored Wars.

So this morning, Ricardo's *Endocrine* had headed straight for the wormhole, puttering past the station at impulse speed. It was as fast as they dared go, since GS9 was in a "slow—no wake" zone. And for a while it seemed that their gamble had paid off, since they'd been making good time. But in the past hour, everyone on the Bridge—even Piker—had begun to suspect that making good time didn't count for much if you weren't really getting anywhere. To make matters worse, gas stations in the Gummi Quadrant were few and far between.

"We haven't been on course since we hit that construction detour," Troit persisted. "Maybe one of the locals can help us find the main route again. Look, there's a postal freighter. Why don't we flag it down and ask for directions?"

Ricardo set his jaw firmly. "We don't need to ask for directions because we are not lost," he insisted. He turned his back on Troit and addressed Piker: "Number One, that map may show only the *old* route numbers, as you claim, but surely there are *some* landmarks to help us locate our position."

Piker turned the map upside down, squinted at it, turned it sideways, and squinted harder. "I'm not sure," he said finally. "I think we're close to the Gummi Quadrant's western border, so any minute now we should cross this sidewalk." He thrust the map forward for Ricardo's inspection.

Ricardo followed Piker's pointing finger to the "sidewalk"—the grid of coordinates bordering the map's edge. Ricardo remained silent, but something about the look in his eyes made Piker withdraw the map and clumsily try to fold it.

"I wish you'd stop being so silly," Troit remarked. "What is this macho thing that makes men refuse to ask for directions?"

Ricardo's face reddened, but again he refused to answer her.

"Captain," said Wart from his Tactical station, "sensors indicate that we are running low on fuel. Nearest known refueling station is back at Geek Space Nine."

"Captain Ricardo," Chief Engineer Georgie LaForgery's voice came over the intercom from Engineering, "the fratzenjammer molecules in this quadrant are making the sprucer inducer run really hard. Either we find a place to pick up some fuel thinner or the engine will pop a gasket."

"All right!" Capt. Ricardo shouted, standing up and

stomping his foot. "You win! We're lost! We've blown it!" He thrust his arms upward in a gesture of futility. "The first phase of this mission is kaput! We'll go back to Geek Space Nine and start over!"

He paused to catch his breath. Everyone stared at him. "Well?" he demanded. "Are you happy now?"

There was a long silence. Finally Counselor Troit stated, "No, they're not happy. They're afraid their captain has lost his mind."

"That was not a request for a Betavoid analysis, Counselor," Ricardo replied icily. "It was a rhetorical question."

"I'm aware of that, Captain," she replied with equal chilliness. "May I see you in your Ready Room, please?"

Without waiting for his response, Troit headed for the Ready Room door at the side of the Bridge. Reluctantly, Ricardo followed. Piker and Wart raised their eyebrows and exchanged a "whoa—get a load of *her*" glance.

As soon as Ricardo seated himself behind his desk, Troit came to the point. "Captain," she said, "as Ship's Shrink, I'm charged with evaluating the mental and emotional balance of the crew. It's my duty to speak out if one of the senior officers should behave in an unstable manner."

Ricardo appeared to brace himself as Troit went on, "With all due respect, sir . . ." She paused, then plunged ahead, "I think that lately you've had too much caffeine."

Captain Ricardo drew in a long, careful breath. "That's a very serious charge, Counselor," he responded solemnly, resting his elbows on the desk and steepling his fingers in front of his mouth.

"Yes, Captain," Troit answered. "I'm aware of the possible ramifications."

"And do you have any proof to back up this allegation?"

"Yes, sir," said Troit. "The databanks of the replicators show that you're drinking, on average, sixteen cups of Earl Grape tea each day."

"Really?" Ricardo said. "That many?" He drummed his fingers on the desktop. "I had no idea." Ricardo began rocking back and forth in his chair. "Well, one needs one's little vices to get through the day, doesn't one?"

Troit frowned. "I really think the situation has gotten out of hand, Captain. I recommend that you cut down to no more than three cups a day."

"Three cups?" Ricardo echoed in disbelief. "Oh, come on, Deanna, that's absurd. Look, if my tea drinking were really a problem, the caffeine would be keeping me awake, wouldn't it? But I've had no trouble at all sleeping at night."

"It's not your sleeping patterns I'm concerned about," Troit said. "It's the way you tend to fly off the handle lately."

" 'Fly off the handle'? " Ricardo repeated in a near-shout. "Of all the impertinent—" He caught himself and toned down his voice, asking in a honey-smooth tone, "Can you give me an example?"

"Yes," Troit said. "Yesterday when that old woman hurried down the hall to board the Crewmover car we were on, you pressed the 'close door' button and yelled at her to catch the next one."

"I was in a hurry," Ricardo maintained. "Besides, she was just a civilian, not a crewmember."

"But, Captain, her arm was caught in the door—"

"Any other examples, Counselor?" Ricardo interrupted.

"What about earlier this morning, when you scolded Lieutenant Wart for 'breathing too loudly'?"

"The phlegm in his throat was making a tremendous racket," Ricardo asserted. "I'm surprised it didn't get on your nerves, too, since you were sitting right next to me. Perhaps my hearing is better than yours." Seeing that Troit was unconvinced, Ricardo added, "I just wanted him to clear his throat or start breathing through his nose like a normal person, that's all."

Troit shook her head. "I'm sorry, Captain. I know it'll be hard for you. But since you seem to be in deep denial over your problem, I recommend that you cut out tea entirely."

“I just wanted him to clear his throat.”

Capt. Ricardo's eyes shifted around as he seemed to weigh his alternatives. Finally he replied tersely, "Fine. Then that's what I shall do. Thank you for your input, Counselor."

Troit appeared suspicious of his abrupt surrender. "You agree, then? No tea at all? You know that the replicator records will show if you try to sneak some."

"I'm aware of that, Counselor."

Troit gave him one last skeptical glance, then left the room to resume her post on the Bridge.

"Anyway," Ricardo said to himself, "replicator records are made to be broken." He strolled over to the replicator panel on the wall and ordered, "I want to place an off-the-record order, authorization Ricardo-alpha-beta-twenty-three-skidoo. Tea. Earl Grape. Hot."

But instead of materializing a cup of tea in a fast-motion molecular swirl, the replicator sounded an alarm: *Ah-OOOO-gah! Ah-OOOO-gah!*

Scowling, Troit rushed back into the Ready Room.

"Just testing," Ricardo claimed.

A few hours later, after his ship was secured at the docking ring of Geek Space Nine, Capt. Ricardo hurried down the Promenade toward the office of Security Chief Dodo.

Ricardo's crew was running out of options. Their one stroke of luck—that the hostile Cmdr. Crisco was away from the station, taking in a game of donkey baseball on nearby Broccoli-Prime—faded in importance as the problems mounted.

There was an unexplained shortage of Gummi Quadrant maps on the station. They'd all been bought up a few days ago. The crew inquired about travel guides and learned that Major Vera Obese, a native Bridgeoran, was their best bet. Unfortunately, she'd recently taken a personal leave and headed into the Gummi Quadrant.

So now Ricardo was about to approach Dodo, who was

said to be the second-best choice to guide them through the quadrant.

Ricardo knew that Dodo couldn't be charmed into helping them. Dodo hadn't bothered to hide his dislike of the crew during their previous visit. But Ricardo glanced through the personnel files from that mission—*Thank goodness I make a point never to throw away any of the old paperwork,* he thought—and found what could prove to be Dodo's hot button.

Dodo was a shapeshifter. After being discovered on the north side of a tree in the Gummi Quadrant, he'd spent his so-called "formative years" in a laboratory assuming various bloblike shapes. Coached by a scientist who believed that this strange new life form could be more than just a hunk of Silly Putty, Dodo practiced his moves.

The scientist was correct. Dodo now maintained a quasi-human body most of the time but could also imitate anything from a boa constrictor to a toilet plunger when he put his mind to it.

Ever since he'd come into his own, Dodo had been haunted by a longing to meet others of his kind. Apparently he was unaware that outside the Gummi Quadrant, shapeshifters were as common as crabgrass. Ricardo recalled that Westerly Flusher's first love, Saline, and her guardian, Ain'a, were shapeshifters. Captain Smirk had mentioned several encounters with shapeshifters, too, including a whole slew of them on AntHill-4.

However, it was just as well that they'd never discussed the issue with Dodo. Since he was unaware of these other shapeshifters, he'd be much more motivated to consider Ricardo's proposal.

Ricardo fixed a smile on his face as he entered the Security office for his appointment with Dodo. Dodo answered with a cold stare; something about the way Dodo's eyeballs rested deep in their sockets gave Ricardo the creeps.

Ricardo explained his crew's mission and said that Dodo had been highly recommended as a guide because "people

Dodo spent his "formative years" in a laboratory assuming various bloblike shapes.

say you'll understand Laika's mode of operation and help us find her and win her over."

"I don't follow you," Dodo rasped, conveying his annoyance with a frown that was pretty effective, considering his lack of eyebrows.

"Oh, didn't you know?" Ricardo asked, trying to keep his tone light. "Laika is a shapeshifter."

"Really?" Dodo's voice remained level, but the beads of moisture breaking out on his brow betrayed his keen interest. Either that, or he was overdue for a recuperation period in his pail.

"She temporarily took on dog form for the launch," Ricardo said, "because Earth dwellers of that era weren't ready for something so unfamiliar as a shapeshifter. But the secret came out recently. Who knows what forms she's assumed since then? I'll bet she has some wonderful insights into shapeshifting."

"Indeed," Dodo said, his nostrils fluttering with longing. He thumbed through his daybook, trying to appear nonchalant. "Well, I do have several weeks of accumulated vacation time. . . ." He snapped the book shut. "Very well, Captain, I'll guide your ship through the quadrant."

"Jolly good," Ricardo replied. "How soon can you board?"

Dodo fetched his pail from the corner. "I'm ready now."

"No other luggage? You might want a change of clothes."

"Captain, really," Dodo chided. He flash-shapeshifted through a variety of outfits, faster than a Barbie doll in hyperdrive: fur-trimmed parka with boots / bathrobe / swimsuit with scuba mask and flippers / white tie and tails.

"Oh, yes, of course," Ricardo said.

Soon Ricardo's crew was zipping back through the Gummi Quadrant under Dodo's direction. Ignorance was bliss, for Ricardo's crewmembers were unaware that Capt. Smirk was already far ahead of them, hot on Laika's trail, thanks to the guidance of Major Vera Obese and all the maps Smirk could buy on Geek Space Nine.

On Ricardo's ship, official duties were light during this portion of the mission, and two of the senior officers asked for large chunks of personal time off. Both Cmdr. Piker and Lt. Cmdr. Dacron wanted to pursue some long-buried ambitions before this last mission ended.

Piker decided to court Counselor Troit in earnest. Their on-again, off-again romance was the stuff of legend, or at least the stuff of restroom gossip. Piker was determined to make one last try for Troit's hand—and the rest of her, too.

And Dacron, the supposedly emotionless android who'd out-emoted all of his crewmates over the years, asked Dr. Flusher to install the emotion chip that his brother Lycra had left behind. Dacron figured he'd better get the operation done before he lost his Starfreak medical coverage.

Flusher prepared Dacron for the chip-implant procedure in the Sick Bay surgical suite. Troit stood nearby, ready to provide a Betavoid assessment of Dacron's emotional state. Next to Troit stood Piker, ready to provide Troit with the emergency shoulder massage he figured she'd need any minute now.

Preparations went quickly. Dacron was lying on the main bio-bed. Flusher turned him off and attached a ground wire to his navel.

Nurse Alyssa Oongawa propped up Dacron's head with a copy of Webster's Unabridged Dictionary. Nurse Oongawa was able to skip the usual hair-prep routine, for Dacron had a straightforward 'do—unlike most of the female patients, whose hair had to be loosened and brushed until it rippled over their shoulders in lovely incongruity with the sterile conditions of the operating room.

Even for this brain surgery, there was no need to shave Dacron's head. When Flusher opened the port side of Dacron's brain, the hair remained in a clump on the access panel, like grass on a golf divot.

Flusher began explaining the procedure out loud, a

time-honored surgeon's practice aimed at hogging all the attention during an operation.

"We're about to perform a chipoplasty," she announced, "the first attempt to transplant an emotion-producing silicon chip from one android into another. The chip was involuntarily donated when Dacron nuked his brother with a phaser and raided him for spare parts. It has been stored in a paper clip box in Dacron's desk drawer since then. Nurse Oongawa—the chip, please."

Nurse Oongawa extended a petri dish, and Dr. Flusher picked up the chip with a tweezer and held it to the light for inspection. "My," Flusher murmured, "what a marvel of technical engin—*oops*." The chip slipped from between the prongs of the tweezer. Dr. Flusher and Nurse Oongawa dropped to their hands and knees to search for it.

Concern clouded Troit's features. "Do you need some help?"

"No, we're fine," Flusher replied, pulling out the pocket flashlight she kept in her lab coat and shining it around the base of the bio-bed.

Piker squeezed Troit's shoulder, murmuring, "You seem a little tense, Deanna. Maybe I should get the baby oil and—"

"Not now, Wilson," she replied, shrugging off his arm.

"Here it is," Flusher announced. She stood up, holding the chip with the tweezer. "Hmmm. Looks like we picked up a little dust." Flusher puffed up her cheeks and blew on the chip a couple of times. "There! Good as new.

"All right, let's begin the procedure. Nurse Oongawa, turn on the music, please."

Flusher adhered to the "whistle while you work" school of thought that allowed physicians to impose their musical tastes on everyone in the operating room. Nurse Oongawa turned on the stereo FM receiver just in time to catch the beginning of this week's broadcast, the 1,285,735th performance from the Metropelican Opera. After the overture, the tenor launched into an aria. Flusher mentally translated from the Italian as she tinkered with Dacron's brain.

A! mia capezzio,
Abbondanza lamborghini é donna mici.
Ah! my delectable cupcake,
I squeeze your luscious flesh between my palms.

Ravageamente mio tu fleshiana.
You look good enough to eat.

Regrette a repasta momenti.
Too bad I just had lunch.

Concludianini suicidi!
Therefore I will kill myself!

Aaaa-vaaay! Aaaaa-vaaaay! Stiletto duletto!
Nostro exito.
Argh! Arrgghh! This knife is dull!
The end is near.

Ciao.
So long.

"That should do it," Flusher concluded, spraying the shiny metalwork of Dacron's brain with a fixative. "I'm ready to close. The mallet, please." She extended a gloved hand, and Nurse Oongawa slapped into it a rubber mallet. Flusher tapped the edges of Dacron's access panel with the mallet till it was flush with his skull.

"Stand by," Flusher told Counselor Troit. "If this worked, you should start sensing emotion from him immediately." Flusher stripped off her gloves while Nurse Oongawa placed the Sick Bay invoice in Dacron's hand.

Troit closed her eyes, the better to concentrate on Dacron's emerging feelings. "I feel . . . longing," she announced, choosing her words carefully, ". . . an intense craving . . . obsessive desire . . . and lust."

"That can't be from Dacron," Flusher said. "I haven't turned him on yet."

Troit opened her eyes and realized where the feelings were coming from. "Com*man*der," she chided. Piker grinned, arching an eyebrow in reply.

Flusher reached behind Dacron to flick his "on" switch. Immediately the android popped up to a sitting position and scanned the invoice.

"You *must* be *joking*," he cried. "This is robbery!" Anger creased Dacron's mouth into a thin line. He jumped off the table, clutching the bill in his fist right under Flusher's nose. "If you think for one minute that I am going to pay this outrageous bill, you are crazy. I intend to consult a lawyer."

"Lieutenant, please calm down," Nurse Oongawa said, grasping his forearm. "That's just a copy for your records. All of the charges are covered by the Starfreak HMO."

In a flash, Dacron's expression switched from bitterness to delight. "My, my," he crooned, giving Oongawa the once-over, "what have we here? Are you doing anything after work tonight? I could use a post-op checkup."

"I think it worked," Troit observed superfluously.

"He sounds just like his brother Lycra," Piker added.

Dacron turned toward them, his emotional kaleidoscope shifting into another pattern. Paranoia edged his voice as he demanded, "Why were there so many people in here during my operation?"

"I'm here to monitor your emotional state," Troit said.

"And I'm here . . . uh . . . as a friend," Piker said.

Sentiment washed over Dacron's face. "Ohhh," he sighed, suddenly on the edge of tears. "I cannot tell you how much that—" his voice broke; he swallowed once, then concluded unsteadily, ". . . how much that means to me-ee-ee." Bursting into a torrent of sobs, he clutched Piker's shoulder, drenching his comrade's uniform with synthetic tears.

"Oh, brother," Piker muttered.

Dr. Flusher pressed a hippospray against Dacron's neck. "This should slow down those mood swings," she predicted.

"Dacron," Counselor Troit said, "I want you to come to my office for a counseling session right away. You're going to need some guidance in handling all these new emotional experiences."

"Hey, what about our date?" Piker demanded. "You and I were going to have dinner in Ten-Foreplay."

"I'll have to take a rain check, Wilson," Troit told him. Piker flashed her a soulful look, but it was no use; Troit was already steering Dacron toward the door. Dr. Flusher went into her office to dictate some unintelligible notes for transcription.

Piker sulked, slumping against the bio-bed and pulling idly on loose threads in its upholstery as Nurse Oongawa tried to mop the floor around his feet. The opera broadcast continued, matching Piker's dark mood—the tenor was still dying:

> *Corpusculo a la drano,*
> *Il puddle del pedesti.*
> *Non removir la stainata alla d'ruggo.*
> My life's blood drains away,
> Pooling at my feet.
> I'll never get this stain out of the carpet.

Meanwhile, on the other *Endocrine*, Capt. Smirk was weaving a tale so seductive that it raised goosebumps on the arms of Major Vera Obese.

That in itself was nothing new; Smirk's fabled charm could melt an ice princess if need be. But this time his charming narrative wasn't about nights of romance or heights of passion. It was about revenge.

"Oooh, Captain," said Major Vera with a hint of a giggle, "tell me again about what happens right after we catch

Laika." She leaned back against the cushions of the sofa in Smirk's quarters.

"That's when I give you the goods on that Carcinogen commander you've been chasing," Smirk purred, "all the evidence you need to re-open the case against him." Mr. Smock had briefed the captain well, recalling from their previous encounter that Vera was immune to romance. Instead, Smock had advised Capt. Smirk, one had to appeal to her background as a Bridgeoran terrorist.

"And?" Vera prompted with a tight little smile.

"And you'll take Gol Iath to small claims court, where he'll be accused of war crimes against Badger."

Vera's eyes sparkled with excitement as Smirk continued to paint his mental picture. "Thanks to your testimony, Gol Iath will be found guilty of everything from running a Carcinogen concentration camp to tapping into cable television without paying the monthly fee.

"In the end, he'll be convicted, and the punishment—"

"—will be to strip the swastika off his uniform and stomp it to pieces!" Unable to contain her excitement, Vera leapt up, thrusting her fist forward. "Yes! I'll crush him! Vengeance is mine! Let his blood be on me and on my children, if I ever have any!"

The flash in Vera's eyes and the wild flapping of her Bridgeoran ear-chain aroused Smirk's romantic instincts. Forgetting Smock's warning, Smirk grabbed Vera by the shoulders and planted a kiss on her lips.

Vera's eyes widened in horror. She broke free of his embrace.

"How dare you make a pass at me!" Vera cried. She cocked her fist and hammered Smirk's jaw with a solid *thwack*. Smirk staggered backward, gaping at her.

"What's the matter?" Vera demanded. "Hasn't any woman ever turned you down before?"

Smirk gingerly touched his jaw, assessing the damage. "Once in a while," he said lightly, "but most of them are a little more subtle."

Smirk followed Vera to the doorway and watched her storm down the corridor.

"Well, I'm not!" Vera stomped out of the room.

Despite the throbbing pain, Smirk followed Vera to the doorway and watched her storm down the corridor. Something about Vera excited him in a way he hadn't felt for ages. She was a real firebrand, the genuine article.

There was a word for Vera, Smirk decided, a word that Mr. Smock used often. "Fascinating," Smirk murmured, shaking his head in admiration. He held on to consciousness until Major Vera disappeared from sight. Then he passed out, smitten with love and the pain of Vera's sock in the jaw.

3

Laika
Rolling Stone

TEA. EARL GRAPE. HOT. The perfect beverage to kick off the morning. Capt. Ricardo took a long sip, swirled the tea over his tongue, and swallowed. The tea did not disappoint: a jolt of caffeine sent tingles all the way from his forehead down through his fingertips and toes. On this morning, in particular, his ultra-sensitivity to caffeine seemed an asset, not a liability.

The others on the Bridge pretended not to notice as Ricardo took another sip from the 32-ounce plastic mug. He'd just purchased it at Chuck's Dilithium Gas & Snack Stop, deep within the Gummi Quadrant.

Ricardo had instructed Dodo to guide them to the refueling station extra early so that he could sneak a cup of tea before Counselor Troit reported for duty. Each morning, Troit spent an hour with Lt. Wart studying *Kr'zhqp-Bltkxvkkk*, an ancient Kringle martial art that employed balance, concentration, fluid movements, and concealed disruptor weapons.

Unfortunately, Ricardo didn't know that Troit's lesson had been canceled that morning; Wart had an appointment with the barber to get his hair straightened. When the Crewmover door whooshed open and Troit, unexpectedly early, strode down the ramp to the center of the Bridge, Ricardo barely had time to thrust the mug of tea behind his

He'd purchased it at Chuck's Dilithium Gas & Snack Shop.

back. He leaned against it to try holding it upright, cursing himself for not spending the extra 39 cents for a non-spill travel lid.

"Good morning, Captain," Troit chirped, taking her seat on his left.

"Good morning, Counsel-*errk!*" Ricardo's voice involuntarily rose on the last syllable as the ship hit turbulence and the mug shifted behind his back. "Ensign, find us some clear air, would you?" he told the crewmember at the Conn station.

"I'm trying, sir," said that morning's Conn operator, Ensign Goldie Retriever, "but it'll be difficult to steer around this choppiness and still stay on course."

Dodo spoke up from the back of the Bridge. "I'm afraid we're in for a bumpy ride, Captain," he said. "This sector is full of air pockets. There's no way around them."

"Very well." Ricardo clenched his teeth as the mug shifted another few degrees to the side. A trickle of scalding tea soaked through his tunic, puddling at the base of his boxer shorts.

Whomp-whomp-whomp. The ship hit turbulence again. More hot tea splashed onto Ricardo's backside. He clasped his left hand over the side of his face to hide a grimace from Counselor Troit.

To Ricardo's right sat Cmdr. Piker, clutching the arm of his command chair to steady himself as he stared admiringly at Counselor Troit. Since he'd first started sharing the Bridge with Troit, Piker had grown to love turbulence for the special bounce it gave her.

Piker's relationship with Troit stretched way back into the years before they joined the *Endocrine* crew. They met at a Starfreak Academy extension campus, where Troit was studying for her master's in counseling and Piker was taking Remedial Astronomy.

Their romance flowered. He bought her flimsy little numbers from the Victoria's Secret catalog; she helped him earn extra credit for class by building a mobile of Earth's solar system. Her affectionate nickname for Piker was *Imsoggy*, a Betavoid term meaning "dumb but lovable oaf." They developed the sort of compatibility that lets lovers finish each other's sentences; mostly, she finished his, since he often lost his train of thought midway through.

But it all ended abruptly when Piker let his career success go to his head. One day he went out to the convenience store to buy a package of Twinkies and never came back. Two weeks later, Troit got his postcard telling her he'd joined the crew of a starship charting the Queasy Quadrant.

When they finally met again upon being posted to the *Endocrine*, they'd grown apart. Piker, whose IQ had risen a few points in the interim, looked up *Imsoggy* in the dictionary and felt vaguely insulted. For her part, Troit reasoned that it was unwise to fraternize with a fellow officer, especially one who outranked her and had complete control over her vacation schedule.

There were still flares of passion, to be sure—here a romp on the carpet amid the poker chips, there a fling of teenybopper lust under the influence of Fountain of Youth water. But such episodes required Troit to take leave of her senses temporarily, and they always left her with a hangover of regret and embarrassment.

Whomp-whomp-whomp. More turbulence. At the front of the Bridge, Lt. Cmdr. Dacron braced himself against his Oops console. When the bumping subsided for a moment, he set the controls to Automatic and closed his eyes to practice dabbling in his newfound emotions.

Irritation was the easiest. All he had to do was recall a few television commercials.

Anxiety was a little trickier. Eventually, by speculating about the crew's impending layoff, he found that he could make his palms sweat.

Love, he knew, would be the hardest. The night before, he'd worked for hours to get it right, with no success. He decided to try it again now.

First he pondered *agape*, the ancient concept of all-accepting love for humankind, but he couldn't get beyond the mental images of crewmates' pranks—like holding a magnet behind his head to make his eyes cross, or forcing his finger into a socket so his hair would stand on end. Harmless little incidents like these had left a trace of resentment. Perhaps *agape* was beyond his capabilities at the moment.

Then Dacron tried to recall what sensual love felt like. He hadn't had such an encounter in years. His social isolation confronted him whenever he scanned the "personals" columns of the tabloid *Starfreak Singles*; his ad was still the only one in the category "androids seeking androids."

Nevertheless, Dacron wasn't entirely naive in this department. A long-ago encounter with crewmate Yasha Tar had been hot enough to blow several fuses in his positronic matrix.

Yet while those gymnastics had been pleasant, something told Dacron that they were merely salsa on the enchilada of true love. The memory of a more fulfilling affair lurked maddeningly at the edge of his consciousness. Dacron suspected that the memory was buried in his Blooper.DOC file, where he tried to protect embarrassing personal failures from retrieval by his infallible hard drive.

Whomp-whomp-WHOMP. The turbulence bounced Dacron out of his chair. As he picked himself off the floor, he noticed Counselor Troit sitting behind him. The sight of her made a piston in his mechanical heart skip a beat. Suddenly it all fell into place.

For several months after Dacron had become intoxicated with the Fountain of Love water, he and Troit had shared a love nest in Milwaukee. He'd never forget the coziness of their Polish flat . . . the afternoon light filtering through the pavement-level window into their bedroom, where his top bunk was always neatly made and Troit's bottom bunk was piled with stuffed animals . . . the static buzzing of the television during the weather report, as Albert the Alleycat predicted "cooler by the lake today, with lower humidery tomorrow" . . . and the steamy scent of the backyard grill as Troit cooked brats for supper while he read the comics in the Green Sheet.

Yet in the midst of this paradise, their affair had petered out. Once the influence of the fountain's water wore off, Dacron couldn't meet Troit's basic emotional needs. Even her request for a morning peck on the cheek gave him a migraine. Troit hung in there far longer than she had to, trying to lure Dacron back into the spirit of their liaison, but it was hopeless.

Finally, one evening, Dacron came home and found her sitting in the rocker, mindlessly devouring a gallon of chocolate custard from Kopp's. She looked up at him and said simply, "Dacron, I want a divorce." Dacron reminded her that they'd never gotten married, so the breakup was even simpler than she'd expected.

Now, sitting at the Conn, Dacron sneaked another look at Troit and whimpered with longing. All the joints in his body threatened to dissolve into jelly, and a ringing like a cheap alarm clock rattled between his ears. The sensations were even stronger than they'd been last time. Surely this was true love.

Dacron felt a stab of regret over what he'd thrown away. But had he indeed blown it for good? Perhaps Troit still harbored some feeling for him. Months after their breakup, when they'd rejoined their fellow crewmembers back on the ship, he and Troit had shared a friendly drink in Ten-Foreplay. Troit had been sipping her Snapple straight up, and it seemed to go to her head, for she'd whispered sentimentally, "We'll always have Milwaukee."

Dacron glanced back at Troit again and blushed as she caught him looking at her. Her answering smile seemed friendly, but that was all.

Glancing at her watch, Troit walked to Dodo's station at the back of the Bridge. "It's time for our session," she told him. Dodo nodded, pressed a few buttons to store the navigation sequence he'd been plotting, and followed her to the Crewmover.

Once Troit was gone, Ricardo sighed with relief and stood up. His entire backside was drenched. As Ricardo mopped up the pool of tea on his chair, Lt. Wart announced that they were being hailed by Starfreak Command. "On-screen," Ricardo ordered without bothering to face the front.

It was Admiral Culpa. "Oooh," she said, embarrassed on Ricardo's behalf by the unmistakeable sogginess of his uniform. "I'm *so* sorry, Captain."

Red-faced, Ricardo turned to the Viewscreen.

"Oh, I suppose it's nothing to be ashamed of," Culpa went on. "It happens to all of us occasionally as we get on in years." She leaned closer to her Viewscreen monitor and whispered, as if Ricardo were the only one on the Bridge who could hear her, "I have some coupons for Adult Dydees if you want them."

"That won't be necessary, Admiral," Ricardo replied. Behind him, Piker and Wart hung on to the nearest furniture for dear life, valiantly fighting off a laughing fit. Dacron, whose sense of humor was still developing, was spared this difficulty.

"To what do we owe the pleasure of a midday call, Admiral?" Ricardo asked.

"Oh, yes. Thank you for reminding me that I'm paying the regular long-distance rates, Captain. I must hurry." Admiral Culpa sat up straighter, waving an admonishing finger as she told them in a rush, "The taxidermist finished touching up Lassie, and we added her to our Classic Creatures exhibit last week, but she hasn't drawn nearly the crowds we'd hoped for—" Admiral Culpa gasped for breath, "—And we realize we need a *live* animal to increase the attendance, so you'd better get going and find Laika. Is that clear?"

"Yes, Admiral," said Ricardo.

"All right, then. I must go now. Again, I'm sorry about

your . . . your problem, Captain." Adm. Culpa signed off with a pitying look.

Dodo's first counseling session was going well, thanks to the groundwork laid by Counselor Troit. Troit's first few casual conversations with Dodo had done more than welcome him to the ship; they'd encouraged him to trust her.

Now, in his initial session on the shrink's couch, Dodo was already confessing the heartbreak of shapeshifting.

"You have no idea what it's like," he said bitterly, "to look down and notice that your leg is dissolving into a pool of gorp just because you let your attention wander for a minute."

"Mmmm," Troit said. "Go on."

"It takes a lot of energy to maintain this human shape," Dodo said. "Thank goodness we wear clothes. It lets me concentrate on my face and hair and hands—things that show."

"You mean," Troit probed delicately, "that beneath your clothes . . ."

"I'm pretty much like a mannequin," Dodo admitted, "smooth and simple. Of course, I can achieve the proper shape for the other . . . um . . . *parts* when the occasion calls for it. In a locker room, for instance."

"I see," Troit said.

Dodo looked up at her from the couch. "It's so easy to talk to you, Counselor. Perhaps it's because you're half Betavoid. I've never completely trusted humans. They always betray me eventually."

Troit wondered, *What will he feel when he learns we lied to him about Laika being a shapeshifter?* She decided to move the discussion to a safer topic.

"Tell me, Dodo," she inquired, "have you ever had a dream about killing your father and marrying your mother?"

* * *

"That Smirk is *such* a sexist creep! I can't stand him!"

Over on Capt. Smirk's ship, much deeper into the Gummi Quadrant than Ricardo's, Major Vera Obese paced back and forth over the orange shag carpeting in Yoohoo's living room. Yoohoo sat on the crushed-velvet love seat watching her.

"He seems to think that women only exist so he can seduce them," Vera groused. "How have you been able to work with him all these years?"

Yoohoo shrugged. "I guess I've gotten used to it. It's just his way." She idly studied her fingernails and inquired, "What exactly did the captain say to you?"

"Uggghh," Vera moaned, flopping down on the sofa opposite Yoohoo. "I'm sitting there at the bar minding my own business, right? And he comes up to me and whispers —right in my ear, mind you—'Hey, there, beautiful, why don't you take off those combat boots and let me rub your feet?' Ha!"

"So?" Yoohoo inquired mildly.

" 'So?'!" Vera echoed. "That doesn't strike you as the most offensive and piggish remark you've ever heard?"

Yoohoo shrugged. "I don't think it deserved a black eye."

"He's lucky that's *all* I gave him," Vera maintained.

Yoohoo patted Vera's hand. "Look, honey, you've got to understand Captain Smirk's history. Women usually fall for him like a ton of Dilithium Crystal Vanish. When someone manages to resist his charm, he just takes it as a challenge. I saw it happen with Counselor Troit from Captain Ricardo's crew, and now he seems to feel the same way about you. Indifference turns him on."

"Someone oughta tell him I'm not just indifferent," Vera said. "I hate his guts."

"That's probably even more of a novelty," Yoohoo pointed out.

"So what are you suggesting? That I pretend to like him, just to get him off my back?"

"No-o-o," Yoohoo said slowly, considering the thought, "by now it's probably too late for that."

"Then what do I do?"

They were interrupted by the weird old-fashioned naval whistle that still preceded intercom announcements on Smirk's ship. "Attention, all hands," came Smirk's voice over the speaker. "We have caught up to Laika's capsule. All senior officers and"—Smirk's tone turned olive-oily—"beautiful Bridgeorans should report to the Bridge immediately. Smirk out."

"Laika is just at the edge of our communicator's range, Captain," Yoohoo reported from her Bridge station. "At the moment, we can only make audio contact."

"Hail her," ordered Capt. Smirk from his command chair. Major Vera stood next to him, looking as if she couldn't wait to could get this over with so she could take her classified info and run.

" 'Hey, you' frequencies open, sir," announced Yoohoo. She suddenly realized that it'd been worth putting her career on hold to take this mission, for uttering that classic phrase again was more satisfying than selling an entire Cadillac full of Murray Kay products.

Smirk cleared his throat and mumbled in an aside to Smock, "What do you *say* to a dog, anyway?" Smock shook his head as if he hadn't a clue.

Smirk addressed the intercom. "Hey there, Laika! Visited any good fire hydrants lately?"

"Captain," Smock pointed out, "Laika is a female. She would not use a hydrant."

Smirk waited for a response. Hearing nothing, he asked Yoohoo, "Are we getting through?"

She nodded, then spoke into her headphone mike: "*Spotnik 2*, please respond."

The silence lengthened. Zulu, monitoring his panel, announced, "Laika's capsule is moving away, Captain."

"Well, that's not very polite," Smirk observed jauntily. "Let's follow her. Full impulse power."

Checkout scanned his console. "Da dog's capsule is headink into orbit of dat planet up ahead."

"We'll catch her before she reaches the other side," Smirk predicted.

"I wouldn't do that if I were you, Captain," Vera warned. "That 'planet' is an off-white star."

Mr. Smock looked puzzled. "I do not recall ever hearing that term before, Major."

"No, of course not," Vera said crossly. "Off-white stars are only found in the Gummi Quadrant."

Smock tapped some Viewscreen control buttons, sharpening the image of the star.

"See that telltale dinginess around the edges?" Vera continued. "That's what happens when a former white star goes through too many meteor showers." She turned to Smirk. "We can't take the ship much closer, Captain. Laika's capsule is probably small and light enough to flex within the luminosity of this star, but we'd be fried."

"You mean I can't just charge in after her?" Smirk asked.

"Not unless you want the star to bake your body like a pizza," Vera replied in a smart-aleck tone. Smirk scowled in frustration.

At the back of the Bridge, Checkout pondered the option Vera had presented them. "Wit or witout anchovies?" he asked.

"What do you suggest we do, Major?" Smirk asked.

"Let's just stay within sensor range of Laika's capsule," Vera said. "She'll have to leave orbit eventually. I can chart all the likely routes she might take through this sector."

"All right," Smirk conceded. "In the meantime, let's try to fool her into thinking we've given up and left. We'll hide behind a moon or something and keep an eye on her capsule from there. The minute she starts to move, we'll be on her tail."

Mime's the Word

"TELL ME AGAIN: vich side is 'port,' and vich is 'starboard'?" Checkout asked.

Zulu shook his head in exasperation. "Just take a sharp left at the next meteor," he said.

Zulu and Checkout had temporary charge of the Bridge. Mr. Smock had gone to the math lab to invent some new prime numbers. Capt. Smirk wanted to visit the tanning salon at the same time, and since his better judgment had taken a leave of absence when Vera came on board, he decided that Checkout and Zulu were competent to park the ship and watch for Laika to emerge from hiding.

Zulu leaned back in the captain's command chair, savoring this rare turn at the helm. At his elbow was a compartment labeled "Captain's Personal Storage." Zulu wondered if he dared to sneak a peek into it. Both Checkout at the Conn and Lt. Jack Russell at the Oops station had their backs to him, so Zulu opened the hinged lid. The compartment was crammed with pocket mirrors. Zulu shut the lid and looked up at the Viewscreen again.

A planet loomed ahead of them, its pockmarked surface filling the entire Viewscreen.

"Whoa!" Zulu exclaimed. "What are you doing?"

Checkout swiveled in his seat. "You said you vanted to park, right?"

"Yes, but at the next tourist rest stop, not here. Where are we?"

"I'm not sure," Checkout replied. "I took a shortcut. But dis would make an excellent spy hideout. Look at all dose craters." He pointed to the Viewscreen, then turned back toward Zulu.

"All right," Zulu conceded. "Put the ship down in one of them. But do it gently."

"You don't have to remind me how to land da ship," Checkout said peevishly. Zulu returned his defiant glare. Checkout added, "I've probably logged more hours as a pilot den you. In fact, I—"

"Aaaaaaa!" Zulu screeched, pointing at the Viewscreen. Checkout had let the ship drift, and now a television broadcast tower loomed in front of them. Checkout gasped, slapping at the Conn buttons. Up swooped the ship at a neck-jerking angle. The broadcast tower grazed the ship's soft underbelly, sending electrical sparks along its shell.

"Mayday! Mayday!" Checkout cried.

"Hey, I'm in charge here," Zulu protested. "I'm the only one who gets to say 'mayday.' "

"Ve have lost navigational control," Checkout reported, working the console in a futile attempt to steer. "Ve're goingk down."

They gaped at the Viewscreen as the planet rushed up at them in a terrifying blur. The ship bounced, scraped the ground and skidded for several miles before crashing into an outcropping of rock. Air bags popped out of every flat surface on the Bridge.

About an hour later, Capt. Ricardo's crew arrived in the same sector of space. Not only had Dodo guided them to Laika; he even knew enough to approach the off-white star from the back side. Perhaps their sudden appearance shocked Laika into lowering her guard, for she answered their hail. Seeing the small, scruffy mixed-breed on the Viewscreen evoked strong reactions from the crew.

"Amazing," Ricardo murmured to himself. "The very first space traveler. I wonder what her autograph would bring on the collectors' market."

Dodo gawked at Laika, not even trying to hide his admiration. "Now that's what I call shapeshifting," he commented to no one in particular. "How does she get the ears so perfect?"

"I can see why Starfreak wants her for the museum. She'd be a huge hit. She looks like a cross between Benji and the dog from 'Petticoat Junction,' " said Piker, ever the connoisseur of culture.

"Awww," crooned Counselor Troit. "She's so cuuuuute."

Ricardo took a step toward the Viewscreen, straightened his shoulders and announced in a pretentious tone, "On behalf of the United Federation of Peanuts, we bid you welcome. I am Jean-Lucy Ricardo, captain of the federation starship *Endocrine*. It is an honor and a privilege to meet you at last."

Laika poked her nose up against her own Viewscreen monitor, sniffed around it, then drew back and barked: "Arf!"

"What does that mean?" Ricardo asked.

"Arf! Arf!" Laika continued.

"The universal-translation-thingy must be broken," Piker speculated.

"Perhaps Mr. Dacron can translate for us," Ricardo said. He hailed Dacron, who was taking a break in his quarters, sifting through his garbage cans in an attempt to experience nostalgia.

"Until Dacron gets here," Ricardo muttered to Piker, "let's try to keep Laika occupied."

Piker nodded. "That's quite a cabin you have there, Laika," he said over-cheerfully. "I see you've been doing some remodeling."

Indeed, the cabin was crammed with all sorts of 24th-century gadgets, including a replicator. Laika pressed a paw against the replicator's control pad, and a dog biscuit materialized. The Bridge crew was treated to the sight of Laika chomping into the biscuit, scattering stray bits and pieces with every crunch, then sniffing the floor and gobbling up the crumbs. When every last molecule of dog biscuit was gone, she turned to the Viewscreen again. "Arf!"

"Yes, indeed," Ricardo said, forcing a smile at Laika. "Nothing like the taste of a nice biscuit, is there?" He whispered to Piker, "What's taking Dacron so long?"

"I don't know," Piker muttered back, "but Laika seems to be losing interest in this conversation." Aloud he said, "Computer, play that Christmas song I retrieved from the archives last December." The computer began playback of the version of "Jingle Bells" in which barking dogs carried the melody.

Laika's ears perked up, and she watched her Viewscreen intently. She threw back her head and began to howl. "Ow-wowww! Ow-ooow-ooow!" The din of the melodic yuletide barking and Laika's howling echoed through the Bridge.

The song ended. Laika barked once and extended her paw toward the control pad. The screen went blank.

"Drat!" said Capt. Ricardo. "Mr. Wart, try to re-establish communication." The Viewscreen showed Laika's capsule beginning to move away from them.

"Laika is not answering our hail," Wart reported from his Tactical station. To Wart's left, the Crewmover doors slid open, and Dacron walked onto the Bridge.

"Dacron, where have you been?" Ricardo demanded.

Puzzled, Dacron stopped halfway down the ramp to his chair. "I came as soon as you—"

"Not soon enough," Ricardo snapped. "We had a chance to talk to Laika, and you blew it."

"Sir, I fail to understand how I could be responsible for—"

"Put a lid on it," Ricardo told him. "Take your seat. And try to figure out what's wrong with the universal translator."

"Yes, sir," Dacron replied. He sat at his Oops station, looking android-calm on the outside but churning with resentment on the inside.

The waves of emotion wafting off Dacron were so profound that they made Counselor Troit's eyes water. She decided she needed to get off the Bridge for a while, so she walked back to Dodo's navigational station and invited him to join her for an unscheduled counseling session. The two of them left in the Crewmover.

Ricardo stood up. "I'll be in my Ready Room," he announced. "You have the Bridge, Number One."

As soon as the Ready Room door closed behind him, Ricardo reached behind his sofa and pulled out a Thermos container filled with tea. He'd gotten it from Beverage Flusher during the brunch they'd shared in her quarters.

Ricardo poured a serving into the jug's plastic cap. It wasn't as elegant as the bone china he was accustomed to, but his Earl Grape craving wouldn't wait on ceremony. The tea was extra strong, as he'd requested, and after just a few swallows he felt better.

"Captain," Piker said over the intercom, "we're being hailed by Admiral Culpa."

"Put her on my Viewscreen in here." Ricardo sat down in front of his personal desktop viewer. Admiral Culpa's image appeared.

"Well, Capt. Ricardo," she began, "any luck with Laika?"

"We've contacted her, Admiral, but we couldn't seem to communicate."

"Oh, I'm so sorry. I should have reminded you that she speaks 20th-century Russian. You may have to reprogram your translator."

"We'll get right on it, Admiral," Ricardo said. "In the meantime, I let Laika move away for a bit. She seems to value her personal space very highly."

"I see," said Culpa. "Well, once you're ready to try again, you might get her attention with one of those silent whistles that only dogs can hear. It always works for my basset hound, Liversnap."

Culpa tried to smooth some stray wisps of hair back into her bun. "By the way, we've been simply deluged with offers from dog food manufacturers for the exclusive right to Laika's celebrity endorsement. It seems as if every pet supply company in the galaxy has sent a representative here to Starfreak Headquarters.

"Admiral Gogetter is sorting it all out for me, since this is a marketing matter. He said that your crew will get a portion of the endorsement fee for bringing Laika back alive. It'll be enough for a substantial early-retirement fund."

After Culpa signed off the Viewscreen, Ricardo took his jug of tea over to the fish tank and stared at the creatures swimming lazily around the ceramic "No Fishing" ornament. *Another involuntary retirement*, he thought bitterly. *All those years of toeing the line, of being Captain Goody Two Shoes, and this is my reward. Maybe Smirk had the right idea after all. I should have spent more time chasing women and trashing alien cultures, and let the missions take care of themselves.*

On the other hand, at least I get to retire with my Starfreak annuity, whereas Smirk—whatever became of him, anyway? The rumors say he's a derelict on Debauchery-4, his mind turned to mush from too much synthol-wine, women and song.

Thank goodness my crew doesn't have to deal with Smirk this time around. We've got our hands full capturing Laika without interference from him. Ricardo took a swallow of tea directly from his Thermos jug and leaned on the tank, studying the fish as if they provided the key to his future. Then he opened the lid of the fish tank and sprinkled a portion of Tuna Helper over the water.

Counselor Troit left her office and strode briskly down the corridor, trying to work off some of the excess emotion she'd soaked up during the counseling session with Dodo.

It had been an unusual session. Dodo had been so excited about having seen another shapeshifter—he thought—that he could hardly hold his shape on Troit's couch. Troit found it difficult to concentrate on a patient who kept changing from humanoid to other-oid.

Dodo had babbled on and on about Laika. The more excited he became, the guiltier Troit had felt about her part in the plot to deceive him. She was glad when the time clock buzzed and she could punch out of the session.

Now her walk took her to her quarters, and as she entered her living room, she groaned. The coffee table, credenza and couch overflowed with flowers, candy, perfume, gift baskets, cute stuffed animals and foil balloons. Just that morning she'd cleared out loads of similar junk that Dacron and Piker had given her, but apparently they'd each made a visit since then.

Somehow both of them had obtained the personal access code to her quarters. They seemed to track her whereabouts and sneak in separately to leave gifts whenever she was gone. Sometimes one suitor would trash the gifts just left by the other suitor, like the time Dacron's tourism poster proclaiming "Milwaukee—A Great Place on a Great Lake" was shortened by Piker's cross-outs to "Milwaukee—eat lace on a rake."

Troit began wandering the corridor again, her guilt gland working overtime to accommodate her ambivalence over Piker and Dacron.

I shouldn't be seeing either one of them, she thought. *Dacron's still learning to handle his new emotion chip. As his counselor, I should be guiding him, not mooning over his poetry—even though it's the hottest thing I've read since* The 2478 Cosmopolitan Bedside Astrologer. *What if his courtship behavior is just another fluke? I should have learned my lesson in Milwaukee.*

And sure, Will Piker and I go back a long way, but do I

really want to spend my retirement years with someone whose idea of a good time will be to sit in the Holidaydeck playing poker with the Lennon Sisters?

To complicate matters, lately Troit had found herself hankering to start a family with somebody—anybody. At times her biological clock ticked so loudly that it annoyed people sitting near her in the audience at movies.

It was all so confusing. After taking a deep breath to calm herself, Troit realized that she should solve her professional dilemma before she made any decisions about her personal life.

She headed for the Bridge. *I've got to persuade Capt. Ricardo to let me tell Dodo the truth about Laika. The longer Dodo believes this myth about Laika being a shape-shifter, the more disappointed he'll be when he finally finds out she's just a dog. As a counseling professional, I can't stand by and let him get hurt. There are penalties for that sort of thing. I might even lose some of my continuing-education credits.*

Capt. Ricardo gazed at the kissing gouramis nibbling at the Tuna Helper in his Ready Room fish tank. *Beep-beep boop-boop* went the door chime. "Come," Ricardo called absent-mindedly. The door whisked open, then closed. Someone stepped toward him.

"May I speak to you for a moment, Captain?" The sound of Counselor Troit's voice stabbed Ricardo with a jolt of fear. He clutched the Thermos container of tea to his chest.

"Of course," he replied without turning around. "Take a seat on the couch, Counselor." Ricardo peeked over his shoulder, and as soon as Troit's back was turned, he poured the remaining tea into the fish tank. He barely had time to drop the empty jug behind the potted ficus benjamina next to his desk before Troit turned and sat on the couch.

Ricardo took a chair opposite the couch. "What can I do for you, Deanna?"

Troit explained her qualms about deceiving Dodo. "If

you could let me break the news to him gently, Captain," she concluded, "he might have an easier time accepting the truth. He's got to find out eventually. I hate to think how he'll react if he invests any more hope in this notion that Laika is a shapeshifter."

Something behind Ricardo's shoulder caught Troit's attention. "What's wrong with your fish?" she wondered. The gouramis, immersed in the tea-stained water, were in an Earl Grape state of mind. They dashed around the tank, nipping at each other's fins.

"It must be that new Marina Fish Chow I'm giving them," Ricardo said quickly. "A high-performance diet, you know. Getting back to this matter of Dodo, Counselor," Ricardo said, drawing her attention away from the fish tank, "he will learn the truth about Laika eventually, but now is not the time. We can't find our way through the Gummi Quadrant without him. I'm certain he wouldn't be willing to guide us without this—er—incentive."

"This lie, you mean," Troit countered.

"Don't you get on your high horse with me, Deanna," Ricardo growled. "The entire crew's retirement funding is at stake here. You're to continue letting Dodo think that Laika is a shapeshifter. That's an order."

"Well, you certainly are short-tempered today," Troit observed. "You haven't been nipping at the tea again, have you?"

Before Ricardo could answer, Troit was distracted by splashing in the fish tank. The gouramis, frantically swimming in a circle, had whipped up a whirlpool funnel. "What in the world . . ." Troit said, walking toward the tank to investigate; another two steps and she would bump into the tea jug on the floor.

Just then a sharp jolt rocked the ship, throwing Troit and Ricardo to the floor. The whooping Red Alert horn sounded as red lights flashed at the perimeter of the room. "Thank goodness," Ricardo mumbled. On his way to help

Troit to her feet, he kicked the Thermos container under his desk. The two of them hurried to the Bridge.

"Status, Number One," Ricardo demanded, taking his command chair.

"Sir, I followed a distress signal down to this planet." Piker rubbed a bruise on his forehead. "Sorry about the bumpy landing. The inertial dampers seem to be low on inertia."

"Who's sending the distress signal?" Ricardo asked Lt. Wart.

"Unknown. We have lost the signal," Wart reported. "Our aerial snapped off when we passed under a low tree branch during landing." The Viewscreen was white with static.

"I'm taking an Away Team to investigate," Ricardo said.

"Captain," Piker announced, tugging importantly on his tunic, "I can't let you endanger your safety on an Away Mission. As First Officer, it's my duty to—"

"Yes, I know, I know," Ricardo cut in. "Enough with the technicalities. If I don't get off this ship and breathe some fresh air, I'm going to jump out of my skin. You have the Bridge, Number One. Dacron, Wart, Dodo—come with me." The four of them headed for the Crewmover.

"But what if I don't *want* the Bridge?" Piker muttered. "Why does *he* get to make an exception whenever there's an interesting Away Mission?"

The Crewmover door closed. Piker turned to scowl at it, which brought him face to face with Troit. A thought threatened to occur to him, though it wasn't the lightbulb-over-the-head kind of revelation—more like a candle. Perhaps this situation had its advantages after all, Piker realized. With everyone else gone, he could monopolize Troit's attention. This called for a smooth line to open a dialogue.

"Your eyes look particularly lovely today, Deanna," he told her. "How many pounds of makeup did you put on this morning?"

* * *

The Away Team trudged up a rugged hillside path. As they neared the summit, Ricardo panted, "Something about this . . . place . . . looks familiar." They halted on the pathway to catch their breath.

"That is a possibility," Dacron said, "since this planet was moved to the Gummi Quadrant a few years ago as part of an urban renewal program." Dacron scanned the area for a few moments, then reported, "My memory banks confirm that we have been in this vicinity before."

Dacron, unlike Ricardo, Dodo, and Wart, had been hiking steadily with no shortness of breath to interfere with his blather output. Far from it. "When we cross the next ridge, we will step onto a large plateau overlooking the entire region," Dacron said. "In the middle of the plateau is a collection of patio furniture made of stone. It was to be the site of a peace conference."

"That's . . . where we stood . . . last time?"

"Yes, Captain. We transported to this mountaintop with a mute empath, then left him here. He hoped his presence would attract the warring people of this planet, so that he could lead peace talks in hopes of ending their centuries-old dispute."

"What was his name again?"

"Reebok, sir."

Ricardo nodded. "Ah, yes." They resumed their walk up the path.

"Wait a minute," said Dodo, who was puffing from the exertion. "If this . . . mediator was mute . . . how could he . . . hope to lead . . . the peace talks?"

"By George . . . that's a good question," Ricardo said. "I don't remember."

"I do," Dacron piped up.

"Of course," Wart grumbled.

"Reebok communicated through three translators who read his intentions telepathically and expressed them in words," Dacron continued. "Each translator interpreted a different aspect of Reebok's personality: one for his purely logical thoughts, another for his emotions, and a third for the kind of endorphin-induced schemes a person gets while jogging."

"Oh," said Dodo, huffing and puffing, "so he planned . . . to use these . . . translators . . . to lead the peace talks."

"No," said Dacron. "The translators left Reebok to start their own public relations firm."

Dodo glared, angry with Dacron for making him squander his breath untangling this can of worms. Dodo stopped in the middle of the trail, forcing the others to stop, too. "So how . . . was he going . . . to conduct . . . the talks?"

"After losing his translators, Reebok learned to communicate without them," Dacron said. "Counselor Troit and I taught him the fine art of mime."

Wart and Dodo groaned.

Ricardo flinched. "Now I remember why I was so eager to leave him and get out of here. That mime business."

"What do you mean, Captain?" Dacron asked.

"Mimes—the very idea," Ricardo said with a curl of his lip. "It's like watching someone scraping their fingernails across a blackboard."

"I *hate* mimes," Wart declared.

Dodo gave a cynical chuckle. "Doesn't everybody?"

"I do not," Dacron claimed, his eyebrows raised innocently.

"You haven't run across one since you got emotions," Wart said. "Just wait."

Ricardo shuddered. "Never mind. It was years ago that we left Reebok on the plateau so he could wait for the warring parties to show up. No one is suggesting that we're going to run across him or any other mimes here today." They resumed their climb.

Soon they crested the hill. The plateau, small enough for them to take in at a glance, supported a round stone table, several stone lounge chairs with adjustable backs, and a stone picnic umbrella. In the middle of it all stood a solitary figure.

"No." Ricardo's voice was cold with horror. "It can't be."

"This . . . cannot . . . be . . . happening," Wart said slowly and deliberately, as if trying to wake himself from a nightmare.

Yet it was happening. There was Reebok, staring at them. While they recognized his clothing and his flowing auburn hair, his face was hidden behind a grotesque application of black and white makeup.

"Dacron," Capt. Ricardo said, pushing his second officer forward, "you know some sign language. Go talk to him before he starts doing a routine."

Dacron approached Reebok, and for several minutes the two of them stood at a distance from the others, fingers fluttering in conversation. Dacron returned to the group.

"Reebok said that the warring leaders have not shown up yet," Dacron told Ricardo, "but he believes they are simply stuck in traffic somewhere. In the meantime, he is delighted to have our company, and he would like to entertain us."

Wart grumbled. "I do not like the sound of this." A moment later, Wart's suspicions were confirmed when Reebok turned his profile to the group and leaned forward.

"Look out!" Wart called, throwing himself in front of Ricardo protectively—but not in time to prevent the captain from catching a glimpse of Reebok's routine. Reebok took a step forward, straining against an imaginary force.

"Aaah!" Ricardo cried. "He's doing 'man walking against the wind'!"

"We've got to get away!" Dodo yelled. They sprinted off the plateau and back down the path, occasionally casting fearful glances over their shoulders at Reebok, who stood on the edge of the cliff waving a sign that said "Wait! Come back!"

After reaching the bottom of the hillside path, they sat

for a moment catching their breath. Capt. Ricardo spotted a group of humans coming toward them from a nearby cave. "Dacron, do you recognize any of those people?" he asked. "Are they connected with Reebok in any way?"

Dacron squinted, the better to focus the zoom lenses of his eyeballs on the distant crowd. "I can identify a few of them. They are undesignated personnel who have served on our ship from time to time. Union rules forbade them to speak because we would have had to give them a raise if they did so. Others are unfamiliar to me but appear to be wearing Starfreak uniforms of about 70 years ago. They are all . . ." Dacron hesitated, peering at the group to clarify his vision, ". . . doing some sort of motion with their hands . . ."

"Not something like pretending to feel the surface of a glass box from the inside?" Dodo asked.

"Yes," Dacron said, his voice brightening with sudden insight. "The motion is exactly like that."

The news sent a bolt of terror through his companions.

"More mimes!" Dodo cried.

"I'm outta here!" Wart hollered. Dodo, Wart and Ricardo scrambled away from the advancing strangers.

Dacron followed, catching up to Wart in time to hear the Kringle declare, "I am definitely putting in a request for hazard pay on this mission."

They trotted across a flat valley. "Now I know . . . where we are," Dodo said, gasping for breath. "The Planet of the Mimes. I'd heard about this place . . . but I thought it was . . . just a myth . . . the Bridgeorans made up . . . to scare naughty little kids."

The four sought refuge in a narrow, steep-walled canyon. Their footsteps echoed on the stone path as they hurried down the increasingly slender corridor. Dacron checked his prycorder and announced that the path happened to be a shortcut back to the ship.

The canyon walls grew closer together. The four jogged

“More mimes!” Dodo cried.

faster as a sliver of light up ahead showed them the way out of this shadowy path through the stone. Not far behind, the clatter of footfalls revealed that their pursuers were closing in on them.

"I hear voices ahead," Wart announced.

"That's a good sign," Dodo claimed. "At least we're not about to be ambushed by another pack of mimes."

They pressed on toward the sound. The canyon was so narrow here that they could almost touch the moss-covered walls on both sides. A few steps more and they would be out of the canyon and able to run freely, or perhaps join forces with the noisemakers beyond the opening.

Out they dashed, blinking against the blinding sunlight. Ricardo stopped just in time, nearly running into one of the oncoming figures.

It was Capt. James T. Smirk.

Smirk and Ricardo stood face to face, their jaws dropping open in surprise. "What are *you* doing here?" they cried at once.

"We're escaping some renegade mimes," Ricardo said. "They're about to come through that canyon crevice."

"You, too?" Smirk said. "There's another band chasing *us*." Next to Smirk stood McCaw, still breathing heavily from the run that had led the two of them there.

"Where do these mimes come from?" Ricardo wanted to know.

"A few of them are former crewmembers of mine," Smirk said. "Most of them worked in Security. Pretty dispensable types. Never said anything. Usually got blown away at some point. I had no idea they resented it so much, though. Mr. Smock figures that they've channeled their anger into passive-aggressive behavior. This miming stuff is their way of getting back at us."

Ricardo nodded. "We saw a few people with uniforms like yours in the crowd that's chasing us."

"Look, Jean-Lucy," said Smirk, "it's been fun chatting with you, but we really can't hang around here any longer. It's time to get on with the—er—archeological expedition we came here for."

The beeping of Smirk's two-way radio interrupted him. He flipped open the casing. "Smirk here."

"Cap'n," came the voice of Chief Engineer Snot, "good news. I've fixed the fuzzy capacitor so we can take off. And the radar is working again, too. Mr. Checkout just spotted Laika's capsule."

"Laika's capsule?" Ricardo repeated. As realization dawned, anger screwed his face into a tight pucker, like a cotton blouse tumbling in an overheated dryer at the Laundromat.

Mr. Smock trotted up to them. "Captain," he said, handing Smirk a chrome-covered object, "I have located the mermaid's left bosom. That was the last part of the hood ornament still missing after the crash."

"I guess we'll be going, then. Nice seeing you guys again," Smirk said with a *gotcha!* grin at Ricardo. "Mr. Snot," Smirk said into the radio, "three to beam up." They disappeared in the sparkles of an Ultrafax beam.

"Laika's capsule?!" Ricardo roared in a delayed reaction. "And then they just beam out of here? Why didn't we think of that?"

Dodo glanced over his shoulder and spotted the foremost members of the mime mob bursting out of the canyon opening, doing an on-the-run version of the glass box routine.

"Aaaaah!" Dodo screamed. "Not mimes! Anything but mimes!"

Ricardo pressed his insignia communicator. "*Endocrine*, transport us back immediately," he ordered.

The transporter technician replied, "I can't get a lock on all four of you." Dodo was running in circles.

"Mr. Wart, hold him down long enough for us to transport," Ricardo said. Wart obliged by tackling Dodo and sitting on him as the transport sequence got underway, with Dodo still screaming, "Somebody stop them before they start doing 'Man eating a plate of spaghetti'!"

5

All Counseled Out

LATER THAT DAY, Chief Bartender Guano set a tall glass on the bar in front of Capt. Ricardo. The surface of the drink was smothered in pink froth, from which emerged a tiny scarlet paper umbrella, two oversized purple straws, and a swizzle stick with aqua cellophane frizzies. "Here you are," Guano said. "One Earl Grape tea, incognito."

"Please, Guano—not so loud," Ricardo whispered. For the tenth time, he glanced over his shoulder at the other patrons of the Ten-Foreplay lounge, checking for Counselor Troit's presence.

Dr. Flusher took a seat next to Ricardo. Guano asked, "What can I get you, Doctor?"

"I'll have a banana daiquiri," Flusher ordered.

"*Banana* daiquiri?"

"Yes. Is that a problem, Guano?"

Guano assumed a blank expression. "No. Not at all."

"You do know how to make one, don't you?" Flusher asked, her voice lilting with amusement.

"Of course. Of course I do," Guano said a little too quickly. "Banana daiquiri. Daiquiri plus banana. No sweat. One banana daiquiri coming right up." She dropped out of sight behind the counter.

Flusher turned to Ricardo. "I thought you'd like to

know, Captain, that Dodo is recovering nicely from his Marceauphobia. He responded very well to the hippospray I gave him."

"How soon can he resume his navigational duties so we can get out of this holding pattern we're in?"

"It should be just a few hours."

Ricardo frowned. "We need him as soon as possible, now that we're racing against Smirk's crew as well. Drat!" Ricardo took several swallows of tea. "Now I understand why all the maps on Geek Space Nine were purchased before we got there. Smirk is undoubtedly the one who hired Major Vera Obese as a guide, too."

Ricardo nervously pushed his drink away as Counselor Troit walked in the swinging doors to Ten-Foreplay. Immediately Piker and Dacron appeared on either side of Troit, each of them taking an arm and inviting her to a separate table.

"Here you are." Behind the bar, Guano popped out of nowhere and set a huge blue-and-white delft pitcher in front of Beverage. "Banana daiquiri."

Flusher giggled. "What's this big thing?"

"It's from my collection of antiques," Guano boasted. "I looked high and low to find something big enough for the whole banana for your daiquiri."

Flusher pushed the straw down into the liquid. "Huh? There's something hard in here," she said, poking the straw up and down. She tried to take a sip, but no liquid rose through the straw. "Guano, there must be some chunks of banana in this drink. Is your blender working properly?"

"Blender?" Guano's eyes shifted back and forth. Then understanding lightened her expression; her eyebrows would have risen in surprise, if she'd had any eyebrows. She grabbed Flusher's pitcher. "I'll be right back," Guano promised, disappearing beneath the counter again.

In the far corner, the voices of Dacron and Piker were getting louder. "It's my turn to sit with her." "You're

A terrific jolt jarred the room.

wrong. It's mine." Dacron pulled on Troit's right arm while Piker pulled on her left, like two diners fighting over a wishbone.

Ricardo sighed. "I suppose I'll have to break this up," he said, rising from his barstool—but before he could take a step, a terrific jolt jarred the room, tilting everything one way, then the other. Patrons fell, drinks spilled, and the bar dice bounced to the carpet.

After the ship straightened out, people stood up warily, brushing themselves off and buzzing about what might have caused the disturbance.

Ricardo, who ordinarily was on the Bridge during unexpected shipwide jolts, realized for the first time that the other 990-some persons on the vessel never had a clue about why they'd been bounced out of their chairs or hit their heads on the ceiling. Bridge crewmembers usually found out soon enough, but nobody ever bothered to tell the rest of the crew or their family members.

I guess it's just one of the perks of command, Ricardo told himself. *The underlings don't need to know everything that's communicated to the overlings.* Ricardo touched his communicator insignia. "Bridge, this is the captain. Report."

"Sir," Wart's voice answered, "the ship has been boarded. We have a hostage situation."

"What in blazes is a 'hostage situation'?" Ricardo demanded. "Cut the jargon, Lieutenant. Do you mean someone has taken hostages on the Bridge?"

"No, sir. By 'hostage situation,' I meant that the hijackers are upset about the lack of satisfactory hostage candidates here on the Bridge. So I told them that most of the senior officers are in Ten-Foreplay. Perhaps if you lock the doors before they—"

The rest of Wart's suggestion was drowned out as the hijackers kicked open the doors and stormed into Ten-Foreplay, firing their phasers into the crowd.

"Nobody move!" ordered the foremost figure, who

The hijackers kicked open the doors and stormed into Ten-Foreplay.

looked exactly like Cmdr. Piker on a sexy hair day. There were a few squeals of fright, but bar patrons obediently froze in place. The intruders spread through the room with phasers trained on the customers and checked everybody for weapons.

The Piker lookalike spotted Capt. Ricardo and walked toward him. Many of his consorts followed.

"By Jove," Ricardo whispered to Beverage. "Look at them." They were dead ringers for past and present members of Ricardo's crew.

Ricardo recognized the leader as Cmdr. Piker's double, Todd Piker, created years ago by a photocopier malfunction. The crew had rescued him from an abandoned cubic zirconium mine where he'd been stranded for years. He'd spent some time aboard the ship, fighting with Ricardo's first officer over who was the "real" Piker. Eventually he'd left, realizing that the ship couldn't accommodate two Pikers. In fact, many crewmembers confided to him that the ship had trouble accommodating one Piker.

Another hijacker was the time-travel double of Lt. Yasha Tar, whom Ricardo had sent back to defend the *Endocrine C-Sick*. And then there was Tar's daughter, the product of her unfortunate blind date with a Romanumen commander after the *C-Sick* was captured.

The rest of the hijackers' strike force consisted of dozens of Dacron-mutants who'd been generated by the Holidaydeck over the years.

Todd Piker planted himself directly in front of Capt. Ricardo. "Nice to see you again, Jean-Lucy," he taunted.

"What do you want?" Ricardo demanded.

Todd Piker's features grew cold. "Only what we're entitled to. We want to be regulars. To go on missions all the time, not just pop up occasionally like freaks performing for everybody's amusement."

"Come now, Todd," Ricardo said, switching to his most diplomatic tone. "You know we've enjoyed having all of you on board from time to time. We've tried to cater to your needs and treat you with the same dignity as any other honored guests."

"Big deal," Todd Piker said. "We're still taking over your ship." He turned to face the crowd in the bar. "From now on," he announced, "this vessel belongs to my crew of duplicates. It's no longer the USS *Endocrine*. It will be referred to as the Ship of Duals."

Ricardo's delay would have created the perfect opportunity for Capt. Smirk in his pursuit of Laika. But Smirk was busy blowing it, squandering his time on his obsession with Major Vera Obese.

Zulu and Checkout had charge of Smirk's Bridge once again. While squabbling over whose turn it was to press the little green button on the incinerator to destroy a week's worth of spaceship garbage, they completely missed the chance for another Close Encounter of the Laika Kind. The spacedog's capsule left orbit of the off-white star, drifted past their Viewscreen unnoticed, and headed deeper into the Gummi Quadrant.

Smirk was in Sick Bay being treated for a punctured lung.

"You say Major Vera did this to you?" Dr. McCaw crabbed. "What kind of kiss were you trying to plant on her, anyway?"

Capt. Smirk grasped his chest and wheezed, attempting to explain.

"Never mind. I don't want to know," McCaw told him. "Hold still while I mend the damage." He passed a blinking instrument across Smirk's chest.

"Captain," Mr. Smock said solemnly, "I feel it is my duty to inform you that in spending so much time in the romantic pursuit of Major Vera, you are neglecting our mission to capture Laika."

"Mission, schmission," gasped Smirk.

"Hold still!" McCaw ordered, clutching Smirk's shoulder. "If you don't behave, you won't get a Tootsie Roll Pop when I'm done." He turned up the setting and waved the instrument over Smirk's chest again. "Smock has a point, you know," McCaw told the captain. "And chasing Vera hasn't exactly done wonders for your health. Her ladylike resistance to your advances is going to land you in my intensive care ward eventually." He turned off the instrument. "There. How does that feel?"

Smirk took a deep breath. "Much better," he said. "Good job, Moans."

"And as to our suggestions, Captain . . . ?" Smock said, raising an eyebrow questioningly.

"Noted," Smirk said, hopping off the examination table. "And filed for future reference." He tapped his forehead.

"In other words," McCaw said, "ignored."

"Don't worry about me, fellas," Smirk said, re-fastening the front flap of his uniform. "Vera just needs to vent her anger over the way those Carcinogens beat up on her people. I'm willing to be her punching bag for the time being." Smirk got a faraway look in his eyes and murmured, "What a wildcat woman."

Strolling toward the Sick Bay exit, he continued, "Anyway, once she leads us to Laika, and I give her the evidence she needs to press charges against this Carcinogen commander, she'll be like putty in my hands." Smirk halted in the doorway. "Computer, where is Major Vera?"

"Major Vera is in Holidaydeck Three," the computer said, "conducting target practice with disruptor weapons."

"Gentlemen, I'm off to Holidaydeck Three," Smirk announced, "where my little love bug awaits."

The situation in Ricardo's Ten-Foreplay was getting desperate. The hijackers refused to let in medical personnel to treat victims of phaser burns and bar-dice bruises. Everyone's nerves were frazzled after several hours of listening to babies crying, along with the occasional wail from a senior officer. Kookoo O'Brine was lying on her back with the contractions coming two minutes apart, which mystified everyone, since she hadn't been pregnant when she came on board at Geek Space Nine a week before. To top it all off, they were running out of beer nuts.

Capt. Ricardo was about to concede that Todd Piker could call this the Ship of Duals if he wanted to when suddenly Todd and all his cohorts disappeared in an Ultrafax transporter beam.

From the Bridge, Wart inquired over the intercom, "Captain, is everything all right?"

"Yes, Mr. Wart. What happened?"

"Dodo joined me on the Bridge, sir, and reminded me that we could simply beam the intruders back to their ship. I will now destroy the ship with a futon torpedo."

"Wait, Mr. Wart," Ricardo said. "Just delay them somehow till we can get away. Don't destroy them. You never know when we might want to bring back those freaks and parade them around for everyone's amusement."

"All right, everybody," Ricardo urged the Bridge crew several hours later. "This is our best opportunity yet. Let's not waste it."

Laika had just answered their hail again, and this time, Ricardo felt, the crew was much better prepared. Dacron sat at his station with a thick electrical cord connecting his brain to the ship's computer. Chief Engineer Georgie LaForgery and a brilliant rookie engineer, Ensign Gordon Setter, had rigged up this connection. It made Dacron a barking interface between Laika and the computer's 20th-century-Russian memory banks.

Laika woofed at them from the Viewscreen. Dacron's eyeballs shifted from side to side. "Arf!" Dacron responded.

"Arf?" answered Laika, cocking her head at him.

"Arf! Arf!" said Dacron.

They exchanged barks, woofs and howls for several minutes. Occasionally Dacron paused to translate for Capt. Ricardo.

It made Dacron a barking interface between Laika and the computer.

"She is not interested in becoming a celebrity if it means being confined to the museum," he reported at one point.

"Tell her about the endorsement offers from the dog food manufacturers," Ricardo urged. "They'd probably give her a lifetime supply of biscuits if she'll surrender."

"Arf arf, arf, wooowooo," Dacron translated. "Grrrowff ruh-ruh-ruh rarf."

Laika responded by tapping her replicator with her paw, then yapping at Dacron.

"She says she already gets all the biscuits she needs from her replicator," Dacron reported.

Dodo stood at the rear of the Bridge, shapeshifting rapidly to attract Laika's attention. He metamorphosed into a flashing neon sign that said "Shapeshifters Rule," but after a glance at him, Laika resumed her conversation with Dacron. Next Dodo showed off his versatility by becoming an outdoor gas barbecue grill cooking a picnic supper, but he shifted abruptly out of that display as Wart, drooling with hunger, made a grab for his hot dog. Finally, summoning forth all his concentration for a special two-creature display, Dodo appeared as a remora latched onto the underside of a shark. Still Laika failed to acknowledge him. He lapsed into Dodo-osity again and sulked at his station.

"Raff rowrf arf-arf," Dacron said.

"Arf arf, ruff ruff," Laika replied, ending the transmission. The Viewscreen showed her capsule moving away.

"What happened?" Ricardo demanded.

"She has to go now," Dacron reported. "Her sensors have picked up a kitty freighter in this sector. She intends to pursue it."

"What about going back to the museum with us?"

"She is simply not interested, Captain," said Dacron.

"Well, *make* her be interested, confound it!" Ricardo hollered. "This is the second time you've blown our chances with her, Lieutenant. Can't you do anything right?"

The remark triggered a synergy between Dacron's exhaustive memory and his newly-honed sense of resentment. The humiliation of being asked to exchange barks with Laika, he realized, was just the latest in a series of ridiculous translation assignments he'd been given over the years. Time and again, the crew had hooked up his brain to various devices that allowed a parade of aliens to use him as a mouthpiece.

Dacron sprang to his feet. "Yes, I can do something right," he told Ricardo. "I can end this exploitation here and now."

Dacron turned on his heel and stomped toward the Crewmover. Unfortunately for his dignity, the electrical cord was still plugged into his left temporal lobe. When he reached the cord's end, it yanked free of the wall outlet, sending a surge of power feedback up toward his brain.

The surge exploded over Dacron's head in a shower of sparks that looked like a miniature fireworks display. "Oooooh," he said, viewing the fireworks with a stunned expression. "Aaaaah."

Times like this make me wonder why I ever went into the counseling profession, Troit thought. *I should have taken my mother's advice and become a dental hygienist.*

Confronted by two patients with equally urgent needs, Troit was attempting a rare dual-patient session. Stretched out on the couch at her right elbow was Dodo. At her left elbow was Dacron, lying on the hide-a-couch that was usually disguised as a bed.

Both of them were pouring out their hearts at the same time. Troit tried to devote an ear to each patient, but their words and emotions overlapped in confusing ways.

"It's so frustrating to finally see another shapeshifter," Dodo said, "and not be able to speak to her."

Simultaneously, Dacron said, "Captain Ricardo seems to think I am merely a telephone receiver he can plug in at his convenience. It makes me so angry that sometimes I

Troit was attempting a rare dual-patient session.

have to press the 'mute' button under my jaw so that he will not hear me talking back to him."

Dodo said, "Why did Laika ignore me? I know she saw my neon sign, but then she looked away. Is she ashamed of her shapeshifting nature? Perhaps she's afraid to 'come out' after all these years of masquerading as a dog."

Dacron said, "That may be why I am making so little headway in courting you, Counselor. Perhaps you are unable to see beyond my android surface. Can you adjust your perception of me now that I have acquired nearly every human attribute except acne?"

"Maybe I could be linked to the computer somehow, the way Dacron was, so Laika and I could speak directly."

"Would you like to go out with me sometime?"

"I wonder if I shouldn't just give up and—"

"Dinner? A movie? How about—"

"—to Geek Space Nine and forget this impossible dream of—"

"—the Holidaydeck to re-create the time Hanky Yankovic played at the Eagle's Club—"

"—shapeshifting ever again."

"—as we polkaed the night away?"

Troit, unable to keep up with either patient's monologue, interspersed psychobabble between their comments as best she could manage. "You have a lot of issues around resentment. . . . This is not about shapeshifting, it's about your identity. . . . This is not about your identity, it's about your indemnity. . . . You must come to terms with your anger. . . . What do *you* think it means? . . . This is not about space, it's about time. . . . It's about doubt. . . . It's about coming out. . . . It's about sauerkraut. . . . Yes. . . . No. . . . Maybe so."

Judging by their increasingly enthusiastic responses, somehow Troit's two patients had extracted nuggets of encouragement from her generic suggestions.

"Do you really think so?" Dodo asked, looking more eager than Troit had ever seen him.

"Er . . . yes," she faltered, "of course."

At the same time, Dacron exclaimed, "You will?!"

"Um . . . certainly," Troit said.

Dodo and Dacron jumped off their couches. "Thank you so much, Counselor," Dodo said, grasping her hand and pumping a hearty handshake. "You've convinced me that my future is here, helping the crew attract Laika."

As soon as Dodo finished the handshake, Dacron clasped Troit's hand and gave it a courtly kiss. "I await our tryst tomorrow night with breathless anticipation," he said.

Troit waited a moment to make sure they'd both left the corridor. Then she stumbled toward Ten-Foreplay in a daze.

The dual counseling session had strained her Betavoid empathy to the limit; she could barely sense the emotions of the crewmembers passing by in the hallway. In fact, Troit's inner resources were so drained that emotion seemed just a vague concept, a passing fancy easily overruled by reason and logic. *So this is what it feels like to be a CPA,* she realized with sudden clarity.

Entering Ten-Foreplay, Troit gravitated to a corner where Piker sat alone at a table. Some survival instinct told her that if anyone could help her unwind, it would be Piker, who was already pretty unwound himself.

"Deanna." He looked sympathetic as she sat down next to him. "Tough day at work?"

"Yes." She turned toward him in surprise. "How did you know?"

"You've been chewing your nails again."

Troit gazed wryly at her ragged fingernails. "Oh, well. There's plenty more at the manicurist's where those came from."

Piker tilted his glass toward Troit, and she gratefully took a gulp of his Can'tFields Diet Chocolate Fudge soda. She smiled, adding, "You know me so well, Wilson. Better than anyone."

He smiled back. "Right now I think you need to forget

Troit knew that other people in the bar were staring, but she didn't care.

about work." He set the soda glass on the table and moved his chair next to Troit's. Gazing into her eyes, he rested his hands gently around her waist.

"I see a lovely woman," he murmured, "who needs to let go of the burden of responsibility . . . who needs someone to help her laugh again . . . who needs a good . . . *tickling!*" His fingers tightened under her ribcage, Troit's most vulnerable tickle zone.

"Aaaiiee!" Troit cried with delight. "Hee hee hee hee! Wilson, stop it! Oh! Oh! Hee hee hee hee!"

How wonderful it was to let go, to give in to this giddy release. Troit knew that other people in the bar were staring, but she didn't care. She abandoned herself to a giggle fit. Her gaiety inspiring Piker to his finest tickling technique. They fell to the carpet, laughing, gasping, and rolling over Troit's hairpiece, which came loose during the melee.

6

Ya, Ve Ist Der Lizardmen

CAPT. SMIRK CHECKED his reflection in the shiny black panels of a computer station on the corridor wall, then continued his stroll toward Major Vera's quarters. His left arm cradled a huge heart-shaped box of chocolates, and his right arm held a dozen long-stemmed roses, for Vera had actually invited him over. "We need to talk about things" was all she'd said, but Smirk believed that any encouragement from her represented a major breakthrough.

Rounding a corner, he whistled the tune of "This Could Be the Start of Something Big" and took a deep whiff of the roses. Perfect. What woman could resist?

He rang her door chime. "Come in" he heard Vera say. The door slid open, and Smirk stepped over the threshold —only to be tripped by Vera's outstretched leg.

Smirk pitched forward, exhaling with a decisive "*oonghff!*" when he hit the floor, his face plunging through the cover of the candy box. Rose thorns pierced him as his chest crushed the bouquet.

Vera jumped on Smirk's back and pinned one arm behind him. "Let's talk," she growled.

With his free hand, Smirk peeled a caramel off his lips. "About what?" he gasped.

"About how you've been leading me on for this entire

mission," Vera snarled, jerking his arm painfully. "It's finally occurred to me, Captain, that you're not terribly serious about finding Laika."

"Of course I am," Smirk countered. "That's been the whole point of this mission all along."

"Then how come you keep putting Zulu and Checkout in charge of the Bridge? Those two clowns couldn't follow my navigational coordinates if their lives depended on it." Vera's knees dug into Smirk's back. "I checked the sensor logs, and they've blown at least three chances to engage Laika's capsule again. Well, Captain?" She twisted his arm.

"Aaah!" Smirk cried. "Okay, okay, so maybe I didn't mind if we took a while finding Laika," he admitted. "I thought you and I needed more time to get to know each other before this mission ended."

"How many times do I have to tell you—I don't *want* to get to know you!" Vera screeched, yanking Smirk's arm at an impossible angle.

"Aayyaa!" Smirk shrieked. Agony turned his breathing into a shallow panting. "Vera, dear, I think you've just broken my arm. This pain is different than before. It's not sexy."

"Good," Vera spat out. "I've finally got your attention. Listen, Smirk, I've already helped your crew more than enough. The deal is off. Now tell me that incriminating evidence you promised—the inside dope on Gol Iath."

Smirk twisted, trying to break free. The movement smeared a streak of raspberry cream across his forehead. "But then you'll leave," he protested.

"You're darned right!" Vera exclaimed, dropping Smirk's fractured arm. She picked up his other arm, bending it backward.

"Oh nooo," Smirk moaned. "Vera, please . . ."

"Tell me!" Vera demanded, pushing harder.

The intercom whistled overhead. "Zulu to Captain Smirk."

"What is it?" Smirk asked in a voice tight with pain.

"Captain, we need you on the Bridge. Sensors have picked up a Carcinogen war vessel just ahead. I don't think they have spotted us yet, sir."

"Carcinogens," Vera repeated in an eager whisper.

"Thank you, Mr. Zulu," Smirk said in as normal a tone as he could manage. "I'm on my—oof!" He exhaled sharply as Vera's boot stomped down onto his spine when she charged out the door.

Gingerly, Smirk lifted his broken arm off his back and rested it on a bed of crushed rose petals and mashed chocolates. "I'm on my way," he concluded.

Counselor Troit clinked her champagne glass against Dacron's glass and smiled at the romantic toast he'd just proposed. *For a blind date, this isn't half bad,* she thought. Then she realized that it wasn't exactly a blind date, since she and Dacron already knew each other. What did one call a date that one had accepted unknowingly? A visually impaired date, perhaps.

It didn't matter; Troit was having a marvelous time. Her misgivings over this rendezvous—which she had somehow agreed to during the confusing dual-counseling session—were forgotten the minute Dacron arrived at her quarters with a sweet bouquet of posies.

Dacron softened her up by reading some poetry he had composed for her that morning. Now he pretended to demonstrate the workings of his ancient slide rule. Troit knew it was just a ruse to get close to her, but she didn't mind. Dacron's hands had an almost humanlike warmth this evening. He must have turned up his thermostat.

Dacron's gentle courtliness struck a chord of longing in Troit. Reverberations of the deep bond they'd forged in Milwaukee oozed through her soul like oil through a crankcase.

". . . And by sliding the bar in either direction," Dacron said, gliding Troit's fingers along the ruler, "one can make precise calculations . . ." He faltered as Troit looked up from the slide rule and gazed directly into his eyes.

Dacron was speechless for a moment, a condition so rare that it rattled him as much as Troit's suddenly intimate gaze.

". . . of numbers," Dacron whispered, "that are . . ."

He paused again, as if trying to regain his composure while searching his vocabulary program for a couple of macros to fall back on. Troit's unnerving beauty was short-circuiting his random access memory; the logical seduction sequence he'd memorized earlier was nowhere to be found. He was going to have to wing it.

Dacron clasped both of Troit's hands in his. "The infinite varieties of calculations made possible by this instrument do not nearly approach the number of ways in which I love you, Deanna."

Troit was flooded with tenderness as she realized that of all the people she knew, only Dacron could make a slide rule seem romantic. From somewhere far away came a whooping sound. A red glow surrounded the two of them. For a few seconds Troit fantasized that these were physical manifestations of their passion. Then she realized that the ship had just gone on another Red Alert.

Troit and Dacron reached their stations on the Bridge just as Capt. Ricardo ordered Lt. Wart to open a "hey, you" frequency. A Carcinogen commander appeared on the Viewscreen. Ricardo and Piker stood at the center of the Bridge for a formal introduction.

"Greetings, Commander," said Ricardo. "I am Jean-Lucy Ricardo, captain of the USS *Endocrine*."

The other nodded and introduced himself: "Gol Darnit." He frowned in a way that made his Carcinogen lizard neck seem especially threatening.

Ricardo muttered to Piker, "These Carcinogens all look alike to me. Which one is he? Look up the name."

Piker strolled back to his command station and tried to

appear nonchalant while reaching down for the paperback *Travel Guide to Carcinogen/English Phrases*. He already knew that "Gol" meant "Colonel," so he thumbed through the d's for a translation of the surname.

"Vhat is your ship doing in this sector?" the Carcinogen demanded.

"I might ask you the same thing, Gol Darnit," Ricardo parried, stalling for time.

"You might, but you aren't going to get the chance," the Carcinogen responded. "I'm the one asking der questions here. Und ve have vays of making you talk." He snapped his fingers, and two aides appeared at his side.

"Allow me to introduce my Wiretapping Officer, Herr Strigenz," the commander said, "and my Chief Nosy Officer, Herr Nett. They haff told me that you haff come looking for a dog by the name of Laika. Vhy is she so important to the federation, Captain?"

Ricardo answered stoutly, "That's for me to know and for you to find out."

In a fit of fury, Gol Darnit slapped his riding crop against a console. "That is the wrong answer!" he shouted. "You do not seem to realize, Captain, that you are dealing mit der Carcinogen military! Being spoilsports is our hobby!"

He halted, panting with deep rage. Several scales fell from an angry greenish patch on his neck. Then he declared, "If you do not leave this sector immediately, I vill launch an immediate Ritzkrieg on your ship. You *do* know vhat a Ritzkrieg is, don't you, Captain?"

When Ricardo hesitated, Dacron blurted out, "A swift, violent barrage of Ritz Cracker missiles garnished with pimientos and nitro-glycerine."

"Verrry goot," Gol Darnit said with an arrogant smile. "Your android is quite discerning, Captain."

Piker sidled back to Capt. Ricardo and muttered in his ear, "I found the translation for 'Darnit.' It's 'Klink.' The commander's name is Colonel Klink. Does that give you anything to go on?"

“Ve have vays of making you talk.”

Ricardo shook his head. "Never heard of him," he muttered back. "Try to find out something about his military record or—"

"Stop that vhispering!" Gol Darnit thundered. "I am giving you until the count of ten to leave this sector." He turned to his pilot. "Herr Raizing, bring the ship about."

"Now wait just a moment," protested Capt. Ricardo. "On whose authority—"

"*Eins*," the Carcinogen began counting, slowly and deliberately. "*Zwei*."

At his Tactical station, Wart tinkered with the Viewscreen's new picture-within-a-picture option until the main view showed the Carcinogen ship while Gol Darnit's image occupied one corner.

The Carcinogen vessel had been holding at right angles to the *Endocrine*. Now it turned toward them, revealing a sign plastered above its front windshield: *Have a Rotten Day*.

"*Drei*," continued Gol Darnit.

"That's three," said Piker, who was using his fingers to keep track.

"*Fünf. Sieben*," Gol Darnit said.

Dacron raised his hand like a schoolboy trying to get the teacher's attention. "Excuse me, Gol," he said. "I believe you skipped 'four' and 'six.' "

"*Acht*," Gol Darnit continued.

"Perhaps we should put the shields up," speculated Capt. Ricardo.

Flashes of light appeared along the wings of the Carcinogen vessel and came streaking toward the *Endocrine*. In the next instant, an explosion knocked the Bridge crewmembers off their feet.

"Hey!" protested Cmdr. Piker, cocking his head defiantly as he lay on the floor. "They cheated!"

* * *

Capt. Smirk limped onto his Bridge. Stumbling toward his command chair, he was surprised that the Viewscreen showed the ship wreathed in a cotton-candy-like fog.

"What's this?" he asked. "Where's the Carcinogen ship?"

"Ve're hidingk from it," Checkout informed him. "Major Vera said dat da Carcinogens vould never find us in here."

"Since when do you take orders from Major Vera?" Smirk demanded.

Checkout shrugged. "Dere vere no senior officers—"

"Zulu," Smirk cut in, "where are we?"

"We've taken the ship into a nebulous nebula, Captain," Zulu said. "Major Vera helped us find it. Our presence is undetectable from the outside. She said we could hide here until the Carcinogens leave."

"Well, I don't like it," Smirk said. "It's like sitting in pea soup. What do the sensors show?"

Zulu checked his console panel. "Sensors do not register within this nebula, Captain."

"Great," Smirk griped. "Computer, where is Major Vera?"

"Major Vera is in Shuttlebay Two," the computer responded.

"Shuttlebay Two?" Smirk echoed. "Smirk to Major Vera," he said to the intercom. "Major, what do you think you're doing?"

"What I should have done a long time ago, Captain," she snapped over the intercom. "Getting off this loony crate and back to Geek Space Nine."

"Wait a minute," Smirk said, an undertone of panic wavering beneath his voice. "You can't go. We need you. You have to guide us out of this nebula. And I need you. We can work things out."

"Spare me, Captain," she snarled. "I don't want to hear any more baloney about the pain of your broken heart."

"Fine," Smirk said, grimacing. "I wasn't even thinking about my heart, anyway. My arm seems to be demanding all the attention right now."

"I've gotta go," Vera said. From the background came the sound of a shuttle engine turning over.

"Wait! Don't you want to hear that incriminating evidence about Gol Iath? The stuff that'll let you cook his goose for his crimes against the Bridgeoran refugees?"

Over the revving of the engine, Vera hollered, "I don't believe you have any evidence at all, Captain. I think you made up the whole story."

"No! It's true! Remember that scam a couple of years ago —the group that tried to pass itself off as the famous sweepstakes? Except that they called theirs *Publicans* Clearinghouse? Well, I know somebody who knows somebody whose cousin will testify that Gol Iath was involved in that scheme. Don't you see? You can put him away for years on this technicality—mail fraud!"

The roar of Vera's shuttlecraft engine rattled the intercom.

"Vera, wait. Don't leave me . . ." Smirk pleaded. The room began to spin, and then everything went black.

Blinking, Smirk drifted back to consciousness, catching glimpses of his surroundings: the worn upholstery of the bio-bed he was lying on . . . the shiny bell of a stethoscope, imprinted "Acme Discount Instruments," as Dr. McCaw leaned over him from the left . . . the shelves of knickknacks behind the glass wall of the gift shop adjacent to Sick Bay.

Someone was standing at his right side. Smirk felt a hand close over his, and he smiled.

"Vera," Smirk murmured, squeezing the hand tenderly and lifting it to his lips.

"Ahem," said a deep voice. Slowly it dawned on Smirk that the hand was connected to the armbone, the armbone connected to the shoulderbone, and the shoulderbone belonged to Mr. Smock.

Mr. Smock politely eased his hand away from Smirk's lips. "Captain, Major Vera has left," he reported.

"What about . . . that information . . . I gave her?" Smirk whispered weakly. "About Gol Iath. I thought she'd be . . . so grateful."

"Mister Zulu reports that after you passed out, Vera said she's known about the mail fraud scheme for years."

"Ohhh," said Smirk, his tone sliding downward in defeat.

"I believe she deliberately stranded us in this nebulous nebula," Smock reported in his maddeningly impartial tone. "I also contacted Starfreak Command and spoke to Admiral Culpa, who is overseeing this mission. While she apologizes for our dilemma—in fact, she seemed to want to take personal responsibility for it—she cannot send a rescue team until the beginning of the next fiscal year at the earliest."

Dr. McCaw frowned at Capt. Smirk. "You're lucky you aren't in any worse shape than this," he scolded. "Bopping around the ship with a broken arm—what a derned fool thing to do." McCaw pressed a hippospray against Smirk's neck. "This will ease the pain."

Smirk felt himself drifting off to sleep again. *There must be a silver lining here somewhere*, he speculated. Then he realized what it was. "Moans," he said, his words already blurry with sleepiness, "I think I've earned at least two Tootsie Roll Pops this time."

7

Graceless Under Pressure

CAPT. RICARDO'S CREW was enduring the third night of the Ritzkrieg, and the bombing was at its worst. Not a minute went by without the explosion of a Carcinogen *Ritzweapon* or the hail of pimiento shrapnel against the ship's hull.

A small crowd hid in one of many makeshift bomb shelters in the *Endocrine*'s basement. A single overhead bulb provided meager light as they huddled on the floor, trying to stay warm under thin brown blankets. Occasionally the bomb blasts made the light flicker and triggered a crackle of static on the intercom speaker, adding urgency to Capt. Ricardo's morale-boosting broadcast from Number 10 Ready Room.

"We shall fight in the meteor fields and the constellations," Ricardo proclaimed over the intercom. "We shall fight in the corridors, we shall fight in the nacelles, we shall fight in the saucer section and on the Spare Bridge. We shall defend our starship, whatever the cost may be. We shall never surrender, and we shall not be taking any vacation days until further notice."

Several people groaned in dismay. Georgie scowled, switching on the map-reading light of his visor, the better to scan the front page of the *London Fog*:

Ricardo's crew was enduring the third night of the Ritzkrieg.

War Effort Flops in Carcinogen Theater

Sensor surveillance of the Carcinogen vessel indicates that Starfreak counterattacks have had little effect on the enemy.

Several Carcinogen senior officers, including Herr Ingbone, Herr Ball, and Herr Brained, showed their disdain of the *Endocrine*'s futon torpedo bombardment by playing volleyball on the roof of their ship during the attack.

"I have nothing to offer but blood, toil, tears, mucus, spittle, and sweat," continued Capt. Ricardo's voice. "And I can say with confidence that I'm sweating as much as any of you, if not more. After all, if we lose this war, I'll miss out on a much larger percentage of the finder's fee for Laika than the rest of you will."

Cmdr. Piker squeezed Counselor Troit's shoulder as he drew the blanket closer around them, and she managed a wan smile. The war had given their romance a sense of urgency, drawing all of their shared activities into sharper focus.

Piker was at his best under these conditions. The siege gave him lots of opportunities to stand on the Bridge and strike gallant poses. He also found a way around the rationing system. Despite the widespread shortages of hosiery and sugar, he'd somehow obtained for Deanna a pair of chocolate-covered pantyhose.

Piker wanted to be on the Bridge at this moment, valiantly resisting the assault by cocking his head and clenching his fists, but Capt. Ricardo had ordered the Bridge crew to evacuate the area during all bombing raids. Everyone assumed he was protecting them from the dangers of the fluorescent ceiling; its flickering during the bombardment was enough to drive one mad. But the real reason for Ricardo's evacuation order was to make sure no one walked in on him unexpectedly in Number 10 Ready Room as he drank his black-market Earl Grape tea.

"Stiff upper lip, everyone," Ricardo's intercom speech continued. "Duty calls us to sacrifice for the public good. Remember that our courageous resistance will inspire humankind for years to come, so that if Starfreak and its Commonwealth last for a thousand years, men will still say, 'This was their final hour.' "

Ricardo signed off, and the intercom's Muzak broadcast resumed with a popular wartime song:

There'll be few birds over
The white cliffs of Rover . . .

" 'Their final hour'?" Dr. Flusher repeated. "What kind of rallying cry is that?" Others shrugged, but before anyone else could comment on the speech, the "all clear" sounded. People rose stiffly to their feet and straggled toward the steps to the upper decks.

Troit and Piker ambled to Ten-Foreplay to keep the date they'd set earlier. They were among the first patrons to arrive at the lounge. Guano was just opening up the place, drawing back the blackout curtains at the windows.

They had their choice of seats. Piker led Troit to a secluded corner table for two. After the waitress left with their drink order, Piker commented matter-of-factly, "I've volunteered for the UXC squad."

"Wilson, no!" Troit exclaimed.

UneXploded Cracker duty was the most dangerous shipboard post available. Whenever a live *Ritzveapon* was discovered amid the rubble after a bombing, UXC volunteers were called in. With 10-foot serving tongs, they would lift the volatile bomb into a Tupperware OrdnanceKeeper, where it could be set off safely.

But the serving tongs were unwieldy, and a single slip could trigger an explosion. UXC volunteers constantly put their lives on the line. Each time they were called out, they acknowledged the danger with black humor, speculating whether this would be the mission that would turn them into "toppings for a Carcinogen hors d'oeuvre."

Yet for all of her concern over Piker's safety, Troit also

felt a strange thrill at his willingness to flirt with danger. In the tumult of wartime, his foolhardiness could be mistaken for fatalistic bravery.

Troit's growing admiration for Piker's war-hero status allowed her to overlook other facets of his behavior—like now, as he puffed on his drinking straw, blowing its paper cover at her face. She dunked her own straw into her chocolate milkshake.

Piker slipped from his chair and dropped to one knee, fumbling in his pocket. "Deanna, there's something important . . ." he began. His voice trailed off as he dug deeper into his pocket, muttering, "Where the heck is that darned—"

"Counselor Troit." Dacron's voice broadcast clearly over the intercom speaker above their heads. "Please report to Holidaydeck Three immediately."

"I'm on my way, Dacron," she responded. To the kneeling Piker, whose head was still deeply bowed as he burrowed through his pocket, she added, "I'll be right back, Wilson."

"I thought I . . . ah, here it is." Piker took his hand from his pocket and straightened up, banging his head on the underside of the table. "Ouch! Deanna, wait a minute."

"I'll be right back," she repeated, heading out the door.

Troit had no idea why Dacron had summoned her to the Holidaydeck, so she was all the more stunned when the simulator's doors opened on a Milwaukee-style slice of life.

Here was a replica of the neighborhood restaurant where she and Dacron had gone for a fish fry every Friday. Dacron must have worked on the simulation program for hours; every detail was perfect.

The paneled entryway was jammed with customers awaiting their turns. Beyond them, waitresses bustled between the tables with serving trays of deep fried battered cod, potato pancakes and cole slaw. The red checkered

She was stunned when the simulator's doors opened on a Milwaukee-style slice of life.

SUMMERFEST
MAYOR MAIER
BREWERS
TODAY'S
Fish Fry
Cannibal
Blackened Kringle sausages
Custard Cones
14
TRY OUR KRINGLE SPECIALTIES

tablecloths looked just the way Troit remembered them, and the plastic flower centerpieces were as stunning as ever.

Troit caught a glimpse of Dacron standing near the bar waving at her, and she squeezed her way through the crowd till she was at his side. "Dacron, I had no idea you were planning this," she said, squeezing his hand.

"I know," Dacron said. "I wanted it to be a surprise. In addition, Deanna, I arrived about ninety minutes ago to put in our request for a table so that you would not have to wait a long time here in the bar. I know how much you dislike all the cigarette smoke in the air."

"How thoughtful of you," Troit said with a smile.

The restaurant hostess called out "Dacron, party of two," and they followed her to a table. As they sat down, their waitress plopped two plates of the day's special in front of them. "Enjoy," she called over her shoulder, already heading for the next table.

Dacron flagged down another waitress and ordered a pitcher of Hubble Lite. When it arrived, he poured a tall glass for each of them.

"So," Troit said brightly, "here's to old times."

"And many happy returns," Dacron said, clinking his glass against hers. He took a sip, then set down the beer and reached for the straw breadbasket in the center of the table. He fumbled around in it for a moment before holding it out for her.

"Would you like a piece of rye bread?" Dacron asked. An excited undertone in his voice told Troit that something was going on here. Either this was extraordinary rye bread, or he had another surprise in store for her. His yellow eyes returned her gaze but gave no further clue. She sensed his emotion chip sending out waves of great anticipation.

Troit peeked into the breadbasket. A small black-velvet box rested between the rye slices. With a puzzled frown, she lifted it out and opened it.

"What is—" Troit stopped short as she saw the diamond ring. She gaped at Dacron, who was down on one knee in front of her.

"Deanna," he said, "I believe our compatibility profiles indicate a high probability of success in a marital relationship. Will you marry me?"

Troit's mouth opened and shut several times. It made her seem to be gasping for air, just as she had when a virus had temporarily de-evolved the crew into various primitive creatures—in her case, a guppy.

"Deanna?" Dacron studied her with concern. "Are you all right?"

Troit's heart raced. Now that she held in her hand what she'd longed for all those months in Milwaukee—a little gold band that showed Dacron cared enough to make a commitment—somehow it seemed unreal. Was it too late to pick up the pieces of that broken dream?

"I—I don't know what to say, Dacron," she stuttered, pushing away from the table and standing abruptly. "This is all so sudden."

One half of Troit longed to cry "Yes, I'll marry you" and fling caution to the winds. Another half whispered, "Be careful. The last time you lost your heart to him, he turned colder than the speedskating oval at the Pettit National Ice Center." A third half thought it would be amusing to postpone her answer for a little while to make Dacron sweat it out.

The second and third halves took hold of her. Troit set the jewelry box on the table and replied, "Dacron, I need a minute to think about this. I'll be right back." She maneuvered her way between the tightly packed tables and walked out of the restaurant. Dacron watched her intently.

The waitress stopped by their table. "How's everything here?" she inquired.

"I believe it is satisfactory," Dacron said, "though the outcome remains to be seen."

"Where'd your lady friend go? She hardly touched her pancakes."

"She had to leave for a few moments," Dacron said, "to consider my marriage proposal."

"Well, how about that!" The waitress beamed at him.

Dacron went on, "I believe she was so overwhelmed that she wished to compose herself before saying 'yes,' in order to make the moment as exquisite as possible."

"That's really sweet," said the waitress. "But in the meantime, do you mind if we move her chair over here? We're trying to seat a party of seven."

Troit's mind whirled from the unexpectedness of Dacron's proposal. She was so preoccupied that she didn't realize her feet were carrying her back to Ten-Foreplay until she found herself standing inside the swinging doors. Piker was motioning to her. In a daze, she walked back to their corner table.

"What took you so long?" Piker asked. "Your milkshake was getting warm, so I drank it and ordered another one for you."

"Thank you," Troit murmured, staring out the window at the onrushing stars as she tried to organize her thoughts. When she looked back at him, Piker was kneeling in front of her again and pulling something from his pocket. Troit gasped; it was another diamond ring.

"As I was saying before Dacron so rudely interrupted us," Piker said, reaching for Troit's hand, "Deanna, will you marry me?"

Troit stared at him in shock. Not that getting two marriage proposals within ten minutes was all that unusual for her, but they usually didn't come this frequently from senior officers.

As confusion saturated her brain cells, Troit grappled with the irrelevant considerations popping into her head. *Who would make a better life partner—Wilson Piker, or Dacron? They both have dark hair. Wilson looks much better in a beard. Dacron is left-handed. That could be important someday, couldn't it?*

"I know this is kind of sudden," Piker was saying. "We've only known each other for a decade or so."

Dacron often irritates me with his endless blathering, whereas Wilson is much more succinct; he can usually irritate me with just one or two brainless remarks.

Piker went on, "I'll admit that marriage used to seem intimidating—the need to make a lifetime commitment and all that. But heck, with this war going on, we could be dead next week. So the commitment part doesn't seem like such a big deal anymore."

Dacron's face glows in the dark, which would cut down our electric bill. On the other hand, he goes through handfuls of expensive D-cell batteries every month.

"I don't think you have to worry about how marriage would affect our careers," Piker asserted. "Once Starfreak puts the *Endocrine* on furlough, you can do some freelance counseling. I'll tag along and be the homemaker for a while."

Then again, Wilson would cost much more to feed.

"And you've probably noticed," Piker continued, "that you and I are the two most attractive people on this ship. We'd have some really great-looking children."

Children! Suddenly Troit remembered that having children was an item on her long-term "things to do" list. She knew that Piker was right: these offspring could be outstanding, provided they inherited their brains from her side, not his.

On the other hand, what would it be like to give birth to the child of an android? She saw herself as Mrs. Dacron nine months from now, lying on the birthing bio-bed in Sick Bay and anxiously asking Dr. Flusher: "What is it? A boy? A girl?"

"Neither," Flusher would reply. "It's a droid."

Troit shuddered, emerging from her mini-daydream. The ticking of her biological clock filled her eardrums,

She saw herself as Mrs. Dacron nine months from now.

drowning out any nagging misgivings about Piker, who was staring at her and biting his lip.

"Yes, Wilson," Troit said. "I will marry you."

Troit trudged back down the corridor to the Holidaydeck. This trip was even more agonizing than the last, for instead of grappling with uncertainty over Dacron's marriage proposal, she was searching for a way to turn him down.

The door to Holidaydeck Three slid open on the bustling fish fry scene. Dacron was still sitting at their table, playing with his cole slaw. He perked up when he saw her coming.

Dacron's eager expression confirmed Troit's fear that she was about to break his heart. The thought was unbearable, and she automatically shifted into her counselor mode, rationalizing, *Dacron can learn something valuable from this experience*. This was her old reliable fall-back position whenever she couldn't figure out how to help a patient.

Dacron stood up and helped Troit into her chair, which he had saved from various waitress encroachments. They sat looking at each other for a long moment with the ring box resting on the table between them, and then they reached for it at the same time; Troit's hand got there first. Slowly she closed the hinged cover.

"Dacron," she said brightly, "I know you've been trying to experience the full spectrum of emotion ever since your operation. How about a practice session right now in . . . oh, I don't know . . . maybe . . . rejection and heartache?"

Dacron's eyes shifted from Troit's face to the jewelry box and back again. "Processing," he whispered.

Troit empathically sensed that Dacron's hopes were being crushed like ants at a Kringle picnic, and she knew she owed him an explanation.

"It's not that I'm not fond of you, Dacron." She patted his hand. "But I've decided to marry Commander Piker."

"Commander Piker," Dacron repeated, staring at Troit's

hand. *Is it my imagination,* Troit wondered, *or is there a tinge of green in his yellow eyes?*

"I see," Dacron went on, his voice wavering. "Then I wish the two of you every happiness." Troit sensed that Dacron's statement was sincere, though his insides were torn up like an interstate highway pillaged by road crews in the springtime.

"Well," she said briskly, eager to make a clean break of it and spare him further agony, "I think we should both get back to work."

"Yes," Dacron said. He gestured toward their untouched plates. "Would you like to take home a doggy bag?" Troit shook her head.

Dacron pocketed the ring box and stood up. "Computer, end program," Dacron ordered, and the restaurant disappeared. Their footsteps echoed through the dark and empty Holidaydeck as they approached the bright corridor.

"Dacron," Troit said on impulse, grasping his forearm, "please do me a favor. Stop by Sick Bay and ask Dr. Flusher for some Rust-Oleum caplets. I think the preventive treatment would do you good."

Dacron nodded. He leaned toward Troit and gently kissed her cheek. Then he turned and walked away.

Troit swallowed against the tightening in her throat as she watched him head down the corridor. *Dacron, please take your medication,* she pleaded silently, knowing that his crying on the inside put him at risk of inner rust.

Ka-BOOOOOOM-CRASH-rumble-BOOOOM-kerplooey-shatter-rumble-rumble-clink-clink-clinkclinkclinkclink.

The unexpected explosion of the nearby Carcinogen ship shook the *Endocrine* to its core, stressing every one of its bolts and nuts, especially the nuts among the command staff.

No air raid siren had preceded the blast, so none of the crewmembers were in the bomb shelters. They took the brunt of the blow wherever they were standing. A few lucky ones, like Counselor Troit and Cmdr. Piker, didn't fall over, since they happened to be in a prone position at the time.

A moment later: "Senior officers, report to the Bridge," Capt. Ricardo ordered over the intercom.

The officers emerged in twos and threes from the Crew-mover. "What happened?" Piker demanded, taking his command chair. Ricardo noticed that Piker looked flustered; the pips on his collar were crooked. Troit, too, seemed to be preoccupied. *Good,* Ricardo thought. *Maybe she won't notice the tea I spilled on my tunic during the blast.*

"The Carcinogen ship blew up," Ricardo told Piker, "but I have no idea why."

Wart and Dodo took up stations at the rail behind Ricardo's chair. "Onscreen, Mr. Wart," Ricardo ordered. The Viewscreen image called up by Wart showed the remains of the Carcinogen ship floating by: flotsam, jetsam, and assorted lizard scales. Angling away from them at the far corner of the Viewscreen was a shuttlecraft. "Wart, hail that shuttle," Ricardo said.

In a moment, the image of the shuttle pilot appeared onscreen. "Shuttlecraft pilot, identify yourself," Ricardo ordered.

"What's it to you?" the pilot countered.

"Sir," Piker stage-whispered, "that's Major Vera Obese."

His whispering caught Vera's attention. "Oh, *you* again," she sneered. Piker grimaced, shifting uneasily in his chair.

"Ah, yes, Major Vera," said Capt. Ricardo. "I didn't recognize you. You've changed your hair, haven't you? It's quite . . . orange now."

Vera stared at him.

"Major," Ricardo continued, "do you know anything about the explosion of the Carcinogen ship?"

"Maybe I do, and maybe I don't," Vera returned in a mocking tone.

Ricardo glanced at Counselor Troit, who was holding up the engraved "He's/she's/they're hiding something" sign the print shop had created for her the previous winter when she was suffering from laryngitis.

Major Vera caught sight of Dodo. "What are you doing here?" she asked.

"The same thing as you, apparently—moonlighting on this dog-catchers' mission," Dodo said, "though your role in this seems to have been a lot more destructive, as usual." Dodo gestured at the debris expanding out into space from ground zero. "Are you still working for the Bridgeoran underground, Major? You know that planting bombs aboard Carcinogen ships is forbidden by Article Sixteen of the treaty with the federation."

"Why, Dodo, you're so suspicious," Vera said coyly. "What makes you think it was a bomb? The Carcinogens could have had a natural-gas leak. Or maybe the safety valve failed on one of their sauerkraut vats."

"Confound it," Ricardo muttered, frowning at the remains of the enemy ship floating around them. "Now I'm going to have to file that complicated Form 350-A, 'Enemy Ship Disabled by Unknown Force.' "

"I'm heading back to Geek Space Nine," Vera told Dodo. "Want a ride?"

"No," Dodo replied. "I'm not quitting until I meet Laika in person."

"Suit yourself." Vera ended her transmission. The Viewscreen of the *Endocrine* showed her shuttlecraft banking away at an angle, then powering off in the direction of the wormhole.

"Status, Mr. Smock," said Capt. Smirk, standing in the center of his Bridge.

"The explosion has knocked us free of the nebula, Captain," Smock reported, checking the sensor panel. "Captain Ricardo's ship is nearby."

"Follow them," Smirk ordered. He staggered toward his command chair, grabbed the armrest, and plopped down into the seat. "And straighten out our flight path, would you, Smock? All this bouncing around is making me dizzy."

"Captain, at the moment, we are not moving at all," Smock said.

"Really?" Smirk shook his head and blinked several times. "Then it must be me. Moans just gave me a doozy of a painkiller." Smirk's head bobbed, then popped back up. "Pill was big enough to choke a horse," he remarked as his head drooped again. He rested against the backrest of his chair. "Smock, you have the Bridge," he said, then yawned and added, "Wake me when something important happens."

With Dodo's guidance, Capt. Ricardo's crew came within hailing distance of Laika in less than an hour; but the wily dogstronaut refused to answer their signal, so Ricardo tried a new tactic. He put Dacron's cat, Spot, in a cage on the roof of the *Endocrine*, hoping to snag Laika's killer instinct.

It worked. Laika moved her capsule closer to investigate. The *Endocrine* snared the capsule with a tractor beam and pulled it into a shuttlebay. Immediately, Ricardo contacted Admiral Culpa with news of the capture.

Starfreak Command was jubilant. Admiral Culpa, Admiral Gogetter and other bigwigs arranged a satellite feed from Ricardo's Bridge so that the reclaiming of Laika could be broadcast live on intergalactic TV. They asked Ricardo to hold the dog in the shuttlebay until prime time, giving them a few precious hours to hype the upcoming broadcast.

"Wonderful news, Counselor," Dodo said. He slithered around on Troit's counseling couch like a blob from a Lava Lite. "Too bad you weren't on duty when it happened. Laika has been brought aboard the ship. She'll be escorted to the Bridge at twenty-one-hundred hours for a live Starfreak broadcast. I'm going to meet her at last."

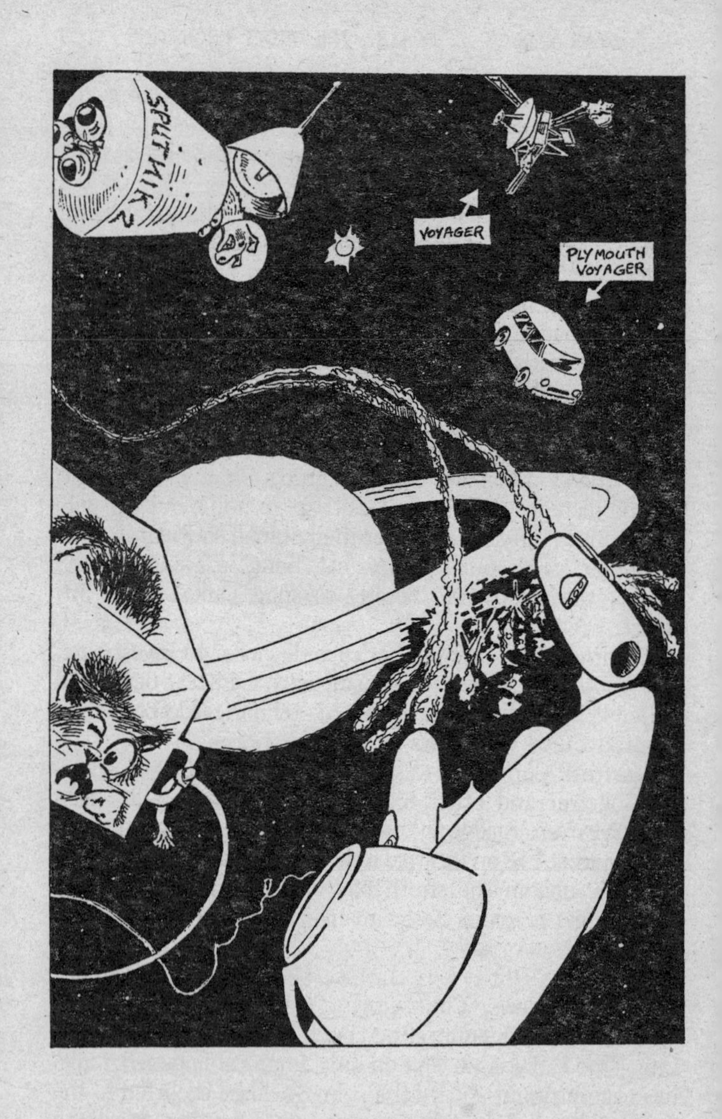

He put Dacron's cat, Spot, in a cage on the roof.

"I see," Troit said, studying Dodo with a look of concern.

"Once she feels she can let down her guard, I'm sure she'll start shapeshifting," Dodo went on. "I wonder what she'll become first?"

"Dodo . . ." Troit said.

Caught up in his excitement, Dodo didn't hear her. "Maybe I should take the lead in shapeshifting. We could do a duet," he speculated. "I become bacon, she becomes eggs. I become a pencil, she becomes an eraser. I become a burning cigarette, she becomes a cancerous lung."

"Dodo." Troit broke in more forcefully this time. "As much as I like to see one of my patients having a breakthrough, this line of thought isn't healthy for you."

"What do you mean, Counselor? I haven't felt this hopeful in a long time."

Troit shook her head. "I'm afraid it's a false hope."

"False?" Dodo was suddenly wary. "Why?"

Troit sighed. For the second time that evening, she had to play the role of pinprick to someone else's balloons of optimism. "Dodo, I think you should know this before the live broadcast. Laika isn't really a shapeshifter. Captain Ricardo made up that story to convince you to come with us. Laika is just a dog. That's all she's ever been."

Troit felt a cauldron of resentment bubbling up inside Dodo as this news sunk in. It boiled over in an intense desire for revenge. Before Troit's astonished eyes, Dodo shapeshifted into a stack of dynamite with a burning fuse. Then he became a sledgehammer. Then he was a cup of Earl Grape tea with a container of poison next to it.

Finally, Dodo turned into a cloud of purple smoke and wafted out of Troit's office through the cold air return near the ceiling.

"A live TV broadcast!" The news roused Capt. Smirk from his stupor. "I want in on that, Mr. Smock. Red Alert!"

Capt. Smirk ordered Smock to devise a plan to sneak him aboard Ricardo's *Endocrine* just as the television transmission was to begin. "We deserve at least as much credit as them," Smirk reasoned. "If they hadn't been following us, they never would have found Laika in the first place."

Mr. Smock began making technical arrangements while Capt. Smirk tended to the other half of the preparation: an emergency session with his barber for a quick wash-and-fluff.

Up on the roof of Ricardo's *Endocrine*, an unseen force lifted Spot's cage and carried it to safety inside the ship. Being a cat, Spot couldn't come right out and show gratitude for the rescue, though she did seem relieved to be able to breathe again.

8

Cry Havoc!—and Let Slip the Dog and Cat of War

"STAND BY, EVERYONE."

The directive sent a brief shiver of stage fright down Ricardo's spine. Suddenly he realized the significance of appearing before an audience of billions on a live television broadcast, during which he would be required to pull off a difficult acting job: pretending fondness for Laika when in reality he hated dogs.

Luckily, Laika was small, so it was easy for Ricardo to hold her in his arms the way Admiral Gogetter, the marketing maven, had advised him a moment ago. "It'll look so much cozier to the home audience," Gogetter had said. "You know—the warm and fuzzy approach."

Laika was certainly warm and fuzzy, though Ricardo preferred his animals a lot colder and smoother, like the fish in his Ready Room tank.

Ricardo and Piker stood in the center of the Bridge facing the Viewscreen, where Admiral Culpa's face now appeared. The monitor off to the side showed the view that the audience was about to see: Admiral Culpa on the left side of the screen, and Ricardo and his Bridge crew on the right.

A flash of UltraFax sparkles at the back of the Bridge caught Ricardo's eye. *That's odd,* he thought. *I don't remember authorizing anyone to UltraFax onto the Bridge*

—especially not now. Then Capt. Smirk solidified within the transporter beam. Before Ricardo could protest, Smirk ducked under the railing and stood next to him.

Over the intercom came the voice of the program director from Starfreak Headquarters: "Three . . . two . . . one . . . we're on." Ricardo glared at Smirk, realizing it was too late to remove him. Then Ricardo gritted his teeth and smiled at the Viewscreen.

Admiral Culpa said, "Good evening, and welcome to a special edition of 'Starfreak Tonight.' We have a wonderful treat in store. We're privileged to have with us Captain Jean-Lucy Ricardo. His starship, the USS *Endocrine,* has rescued the famous Laika, whose capsule was adrift in the Gummi Quadrant. As you'll recall from our mini-series 'Laika, Canine Crusader,' this space pioneer's stellar career has earned her a permanent place in the Starfreak Classic Creatures exhibition of the Milwaukee Public Museum."

"Indeed, Admiral Culpa," Capt. Smirk said, emphasizing his words with his characteristic halting macho-staccato. "And let me say . . . that it was a pleasure . . . to take part . . . in this historic rescue."

"Er—uh—Captain Smirk." Admiral Culpa faltered for a moment, then regained her composure. "Perhaps you'd like to tell us about your role in all of this."

"Certainly, Admiral." Smirk stepped forward, ignoring Ricardo's laser-glare of resentment, which was all but burning a hole in the back of his head. "When my comrade Jean-Lucy asked for guidance through the Gummi Quadrant, I resolved to do everything I could to . . ."

As Smirk strutted his stuff before the camera, the Crewmover door opened. Wart, standing at his Tactical Station, glanced at it. The compartment looked empty at first. Then Wart noticed Dacron's cat, Spot, prancing out onto the Bridge.

Wart stepped toward her. Immediately Spot took off down the ramp and ran across the front of the Bridge, dashing between the captains and the Viewscreen.

The flash of yellow fur and the whiff of feline scent electrified Laika. She leapt out of Ricardo's arms in hot pursuit, barking wildly.

"What the—stop her!" Ricardo hollered.

Laika chased Spot in furious circles around the Bridge. Piker grabbed at them, missed, and crashed into the railing. It collapsed beneath him.

"Spot, heel!" Dacron ordered in his best alpha-animal voice. Spot didn't even slow down.

Wart fired his phaser at the moving targets but succeeded only in wounding Ensign Char Pei at the Conn station.

A pair of shapeshifter eyes popped out of the Crewmover's wallpaper, the better to enjoy this frenzied scene.

"Oh my, oh my," Admiral Culpa fluttered as the live broadcast let the whole galaxy in on this riot.

Laika caught up to Spot. The two merged in a tangle of fur, claws and teeth, rolling around the Bridge. On the far wall, Dacron broke the glass and pulled out the emergency fire hose to spray the animals with cold water. Wart fought his way through the water-stream and picked up Laika. He shoved the dripping animal into Ricardo's arms.

Ricardo stood there stunned for a moment, then realized that he was still on live TV. "Well, Admiral," he said. "What a mission it's been."

Admiral Culpa seemed about to faint. "Captain Ricardo," she fluttered, "what is that in Laika's mouth?"

"Laika's mouth?" Ricardo repeated blankly. He lifted up the dog for closer inspection.

"Oh, my word—" Admiral Culpa gasped, her hands flying to her cheeks, "—it's the cat's tail!"

Admiral Culpa was right. Laika held Spot's tail triumphantly in her mouth. She wagged her own tail as if expecting a compliment for her hunting prowess.

"Cut! Go to commercial, *now!*" the Bridge crew heard the director say over the intercom.

Laika kept on wagging, looking from Ricardo to Smirk

and back again. Smirk ruffled the fur on her neck affectionately.

"Oh my, oh my," Admiral Culpa wheezed. Strands were popping out of her hair-bun right and left.

"Aw, Admiral, you know how it is. Dogs will be dogs," Smirk said philosophically.

"Please hold for a moment, Captains," Culpa said. Her image disappeared from the Viewscreen.

Smirk patted Laika's head. "Attagirl," he told her. "You knew that nasty cat didn't belong on the Bridge, didn't you?"

Dacron addressed the intercom: "Doctor Flusher, please ready an emergency surgical reattachment team at once."

Admiral Culpa reappeared on the Viewscreen.

"Are we back on the air, Admiral?" asked Ricardo.

"No." Admiral Culpa's lips were pursed in disapproval. "And I wish to high heaven we hadn't been on the air a moment ago when this—this—catastrophe occurred. I just fired the director." Smirk and Ricardo tried to look rueful, though each captain was calculating how to pin the blame on the other.

"I consider this an all-time low in Starfreak's public relations," Culpa continued. "Imagine—Starfreak being associated with the mutilation of a poor innocent creature. And the entire galaxy saw it!"

Smirk raised a hand defensively. "Well, I'd hardly call Spot innocent," he began, "the way she was taunting Laika—"

"Captain Smirk! Will you please . . . hush up!" Culpa said, her face reddening. "This is a disaster. Our instant opinion poll shows that Laika's approval rating has plummeted. Who's going to want to see her in the museum now? And advertisers are already pulling out of the arrangements we'd made.

"You know what this means, don't you? There won't be any reward money for any of you. There are no endorsement fees, either. I'm sorry, but . . . no—I'm *not* sorry!"

Admiral Culpa, having delivered the harshest words she was capable of, signed off in a huff.

Ricardo and Smirk glared at each other for a minute, racking their brains for appropriate put-downs, but none came to mind. Ricardo gave up first. "Well," he said flatly, setting Laika down on the carpet. Piker grabbed the dog and boarded the Crewmover with Dacron, who was taking Spot to Sick Bay.

Ricardo lowered himself into his command chair. Smirk sat next to him in Piker's chair. The two rivals seemed remarkably relaxed in each other's company, probably because failing in unison was becoming something of a habit for them.

"So much for *that* mission," Smirk mused.

"You weren't much help," Ricardo growled.

"Huh. It wasn't my cat that barged onto the Bridge, stirring up trouble."

Ricardo grunted.

"A cat on the Bridge—the very idea," Smirk said. "You'd never see that on *my* ship. Here you've got cats, an occasional dog, those fish in your Romper Room, sometimes horses in the Holidaydeck . . . it's practically a flying 4-H."

They were silent for several minutes. Finally Capt. Ricardo said, "Somehow I never thought it would end like this. This was our last mission before being put on furlough, and all I've got to show for it is dog hair all over my tunic."

"It could be worse," Smirk told him. "I have to live with the memory of breaking up with Major Vera. I bet I'll think of her every day for the next five years. It'll take at least that long for the bruises to heal."

A long time later, as dawn crept onto the Bridge and set the robins to chirping, Smirk and Ricardo were still commiserating with each other. Cmdr. Piker approached them.

"Captain Ricardo," Piker said, "I thought you'd want to

know that Laika has left the *Endocrine*. Dodo helped her escape in her shuttlecraft. I think he felt sorry for her."

Ricardo nodded.

"Then Dodo left, too," Piker reported. "He said to thank you for destroying his budding faith in the human race. If you ask me, sir, I think he was being sarcastic."

Ricardo rolled his eyes. "Thank you, Number One. That will be all." Piker cocked his head and strode off the Bridge.

Smirk opened his mouth to begin a new round of griping, but the Viewscreen unexpectedly came on. It was Admiral Gogetter.

"Captains!" he exclaimed. "Great show you guys put on last night! At first it was a little too spontaneous for my nerves, if you catch my drift. But then the ratings came in. They've gone through the roof!"

The captains sat up straighter and leaned toward the Viewscreen.

"The audience loves the idea of you guys out there in space doing your thing, living in the moment and all that," Gogetter raved. "It was so different from the boring weekly broadcast from Geek Space Nine. It was so hot! The viewers want more, more, more! I've been working the phones, and our corporate sponsorship is all lined up."

"Sponsorship? For what, Admiral?" Ricardo asked.

Gogetter beamed at them. "For each of your crews to have its own show. The basic idea is to broadcast your ongoing adventures. We can talk format later. We'll get some input from the focus groups, too. The main thing I want to hear from you tonight is that you're on board with this idea. Are you with me? Do you want to keep on flying those wild and crazy adventures?"

"Count me in," Smirk asserted.

"Er—yes, of course," Ricardo said.

"Cool!" Gogetter exclaimed, and he signed off.

9

United in Holy Gridlock

AN EAGER HUSH HOVERED over Ten-Foreplay as the guests gathered for the wedding of Counselor Troit and Cmdr. Piker. Guano had consented to let them use her lounge on the condition that they order the most expensive items from her catering service. She'd also provided the folding chairs on which the guests were seated, the champagne fountain gently splashing in the corner, and a reflective ball on the ceiling to sparkle light over the dance floor during the reception.

Wart and Georgie LaForgery were the ushers, escorting guests down the aisle after determining whether they belonged on the bride's or the groom's side of the bar. As ushers, they also decided who got a window seat.

Dr. Flusher and Nurse Oongawa sat near the middle, gossiping about the prospects for this marriage.

"It'll never last," predicted Flusher, picking a piece of lint off her formalwear surgical scrubs. "The last couple to hold a wedding here in Ten-Foreplay were Kookoo and Smiles O'Brine, and everybody knows that their marriage is shaky. This place is bad luck."

"What surprised me was when Counselor Troit came in for her prenuptial physical," Nurse Oongawa remarked, "and I found out she's already had a baby."

"Yes, that's right." Flusher nodded as she recalled the

details. "Her pregnancy came to term in just three days. I think you were away at a seminar when it happened. Deanna said that some mysterious alien force entered her while she was asleep. She claimed that's what triggered the conception." Flusher paused, arching her eyebrows at Oongawa. In unison they remarked skeptically, "Yeah, right."

Capt. Smirk and his crew arrived fairly late and chose to sit on the bride's side. Smirk had intended to wear the black armband he usually donned when a former sweetheart got married, but Mr. Smock had dissuaded him.

Within a minute, Smirk began looking around restlessly, squirming in his seat. To keep the captain occupied, Mr. Smock handed him a pencil and a card from the pew racks that Guano had hung from the backs of the chairs. The card read:

Welcome to Guano's (temporary) House of
Worship and Cocktail Lounge

Please fill out this card and hand it to an usher as you leave so that we may have a record of your visit. If you would like the bartender to call on you, check the appropriate boxes below.

Name ________ Rank ____ Serial number ____

Species __________ Starship or planet _________

I would like counseling about:

☐ marital problems ☐ job dissatisfaction

☐ the generally lousy state of the universe

☐ nothing in particular; I just want to cry in my beer

The organist who had been hired for the occasion began playing subdued background music. A minute later the soloist, Woksauna Troit, took her place next to the organ and began warming up by singing scales. Embroidered on the bodice of her lilac crepe gown was the legend "MOTHER of the BRIDE."

Off to one side, Capt. Ricardo, Dacron and Piker emerged from the walk-in beer cooler, which today doubled as a dressing room. Ricardo stood on the makeshift altar where he would officiate the ceremony in accordance with the shipboard tradition that a captain could perform weddings, as well as the Starfreak tradition of keeping the clergy out of things whenever possible.

Dacron, who was Piker's poignant choice to serve as best man, took his place near the altar. His 1960s-style tuxedo, created in the replicator, suited him well; the severe black-and-white color scheme matched his hair and face.

At the center stood Piker, tugging at his collar and casting longing glances at the exit. He wore his dress uniform, an aptly named garment since its tunic looked like a minidress from a 1967 Simplicity Sewing Patterns catalog.

Piker, Dacron and Ricardo fixed their attention on the far end of the aisle of folding chairs. The congregation, sensing that the big moment was at hand, stirred expectantly.

As the organist played the opening chords of the processional, all the guests stood up, the better to see whether the bride would follow Betavoid custom by appearing nude at her wedding.

They were disappointed. Troit wore the traditional gown of white, prompting snickers from Flusher and Oongawa. The gown was fairly modest except for its plunging neckline, but crewmembers were so accustomed to seeing Troit's cleavage day in and day out that this seemed quite mundane.

Woksauna Troit had rewritten the lyrics of "Here Comes the Bride" to reflect her overwhelming relief that her daughter was finally getting married, as well as the openly acknowledged reason for the union. As Deanna stepped down the aisle, Woksauna sang:

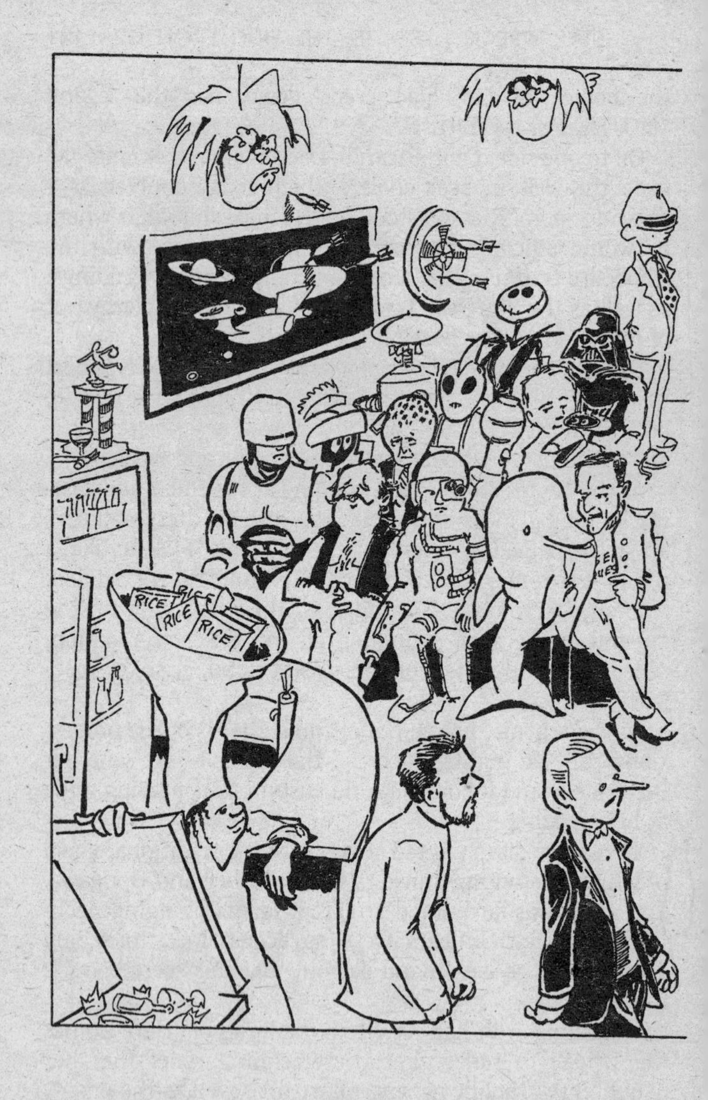

Ricardo, Dacron and Piker emerged from the walk-in beer cooler.

EXIT
REST ROOMS

Here comes the bride.
I'm finally justified.
Here comes the groom.
He'll start a baby boom.

Troit joined Piker at the front, and they turned toward Capt. Ricardo, who began to read the wedding ceremony out of the *Book of Common Palaver*.

"Dear friends," said Ricardo, "we have gathered today to celebrate the union of Deanna and Wilson in holy matrimony. Marriage is an estate that should not be entered into lightly." Out of the side of his mouth, Ricardo muttered, "Goodness knows why you'd want to enter into it at all."

Aloud, he continued, "Today, this man and this woman, being of—" he paused, glancing at Piker, then went on, "sound mind and body, have declared their intention to be united as husband and wife. If there is anyone who knows of any reason why this union should not proceed, let them speak now or forever hold their peace."

A sob escaped Dacron's throat and echoed throughout the makeshift chapel. Piker gave him a dirty look. Dacron pulled himself together, straightening his shoulders and assuming a deadpan expression.

Ricardo turned toward Deanna. "Deanna Vanna Troit, do you take this man to be your lawfully wedded husband, for better or for worse, for richer or for poorer, whether gutted by phaser wounds or ravaged by radiation sickness, and despite any rapidly accumulating mental decline, till death do you part?"

"I do," said Deanna.

Ricardo turned to Piker, who squared his jaw as if he were about to take on a Kringle warrior. "Wilson Pickett Piker, do you take this woman to be your lawfully wedded wife, for better or for worse, for richer or for poorer, for cleavage or for saggage, even if she eventually becomes an old crone like the time that alien diplomat dumped all of his negative emotions into her, till death do you part?"

Despite his painfully obvious effort to follow Ricardo's lengthy question, Piker had lost his train of thought. He scratched his head and asked, "Could you repeat the part about cleavage?"

Troit jabbed an elbow into his ribs, hissing, "Just say 'I do.' "

"I do," Piker echoed obediently.

Ricardo turned to Dacron. "The rings, please."

Dacron searched the inner breast pocket on the left side of his tuxedo jacket. Then he searched the right inner pocket. Then he checked the two outer pockets. Then he checked his pants pockets.

"I seem to have neglected to bring the rings," he observed.

"Freudian slip," Capt. Smirk remarked to Mr. Smock, loud enough for most of the assembly to hear.

Head usher Georgie came to the rescue, scurrying down the aisle. "Here," he whispered to Dacron, pulling from his pocket two rubber gizmos that looked like they belonged in Engineering's junk drawer. "I always carry a few washers with me. You never know when they'll come in handy." Dacron turned them over to Capt. Ricardo.

Ricardo handed a washer to Troit. She repeated after the captain: "Receive this ring as a pledge of my love and faithfulness."

Piker's jitters had gotten worse. As Troit slipped the washer on his finger, Piker's hand trembled so hard that Dacron had to help steady it.

Then it was Piker's turn. Ricardo handed him a washer and indicated that he should put it on Troit's finger. Knowing better than to ask Piker to recite while performing another task, Ricardo waited till the makeshift ring was in place, then read the vow: "Receive this ring as a pledge of my love and faithfulness."

Piker wiped the sweat off his forehead with the back of his hand. "What was that again?"

"Receive this ring as a pledge . . ." Ricardo said.

"Receive the—" Piker began.

"No, not 'receive the.' 'Receive *this*.' "

"Receive . . . uh . . . r-receive . . ." Piker stammered.

"This . . ." Ricardo prompted.

"This . . ." Piker repeated.

"Ring . . ."

"Ring . . ."

"As . . ."

"As . . ."

"A . . ."

"A . . ."

In the rows of folding chairs, the natives were getting restless. Someone made a paper airplane out of the printed wedding program and launched it toward the front, where it landed next to Dacron's dress boot. Woksauna Troit glared out into the congregation, trying to identify the culprit.

Finally Piker made it through the vow. Ricardo instructed Piker and Troit to join hands, then announced, "Since you have declared your love and faithfulness before these witnesses, I therefore pronounce you husband and wife." To Piker he added, "You may kiss the bride."

Piker did so, *con brio*. Then he and his bride marched down the aisle. The organist played the pulsating opening chords of the recessional, chosen by the bridegroom from selections in the archives: the Spencer Davis Group's *Gimme Some Lovin'*.

Immediately, Guano began shouting orders at guests to move the chairs and set up banquet tables. Others were instructed to tape crepe paper streamers to the ceiling. Guano even pulled Dacron out of the reception line for a few minutes and pressed him into service to carry the enormous steam trays to the buffet.

Wart stood off to one side guarding the gift table with a submachine gun. The wrapped packages contained multiple toasters, blenders and spice racks, all of which the newlyweds would later exchange for cash since they planned to keep preparing their meals with a replicator.

Ricardo sauntered up to the champagne fountain, glanced around to see if anyone was watching, and emptied a Thermos container into it. Capt. Smirk startled him by sneaking up and tapping his shoulder. "Spiking the punch, Jean-Lucy?" Smirk asked, dipping the ladle into the bowl and filling a glass for himself.

"It's Earl Grape tea," Ricardo told him. "I've found that a good dose of this in everyone's beverage helps ensure a lively party."

"Mmmph." Already Smirk's attention was wandering. He scanned the guests, hoping to find an attractive stranger he could hit on. Spotting one of Ricardo's new female crew-members standing nearby, Smirk said, "Excuse me. Duty calls."

When the meal was ready, the guests followed the bride and groom down the buffet line. Guano's Catering Service had done a superb job, serving hot foods hot, cold foods cold, and Kringle foods squirming.

In deference to the culinary tastes Troit had acquired as a guest at numerous Milwaukee weddings, the banquet table held a tray of kielbasa and a platter of raw ground beef with onions. Piker filled two dinner plates for himself and balanced a heaping salad plate on top of them.

When everyone was served and seated, Dacron stood up and signaled for quiet. He declared, "In creating a toast for the bride and groom, I have combined an ancient Irish blessing with an old Yiddish nuptial wish." He held up his glass and said, "May the road rise to meet you, may the wind be always at your back, and God willing, you should like each other half as much ten years from now as you do today."

The guests drank to the toast and returned to the serious business of gluttony. A few minutes later, Dr. Flusher be-gan clinking her fork against her glass. "What are you doing?" asked Capt. Smirk, who was seated at her right.

"Deanna once mentioned to me that this was another tradition at Midwestern wedding dinners," Flusher explained. "Every so often, guests tinkle their glasses with silverware, raising a ruckus to get the bride and groom to kiss. I've told some of the other crewmembers about it." Already, these crewmembers had picked up the cue and were likewise striking their glasses with utensils.

"You don't say?" Smirk remarked. He turned to his new-found gorgeous acquaintance, who was seated on his other side. "They have this old tradition," he told her. "Every time you hear that clinking, you're supposed to share a passionate moment with another guest." Smirk draped his arm around her shoulder and pulled her close, kissing her long enough to keep her from noticing that none of the other guests were doing the same.

Ricardo finished his meal early and retired to the Ready Room to entertain callers. One by one, they were escorted into his presence by a Security crewmember. It was an old Starfreak tradition that no captain could refuse a request made on the wedding day of his counselor.

Some of the requests were easy to handle, such as Checkout's need for a Russian-language version of "Hooked on Phonics" and Zulu's search for a rare pair of Teflon-coated chopsticks. Others were considerably more difficult. Snot wanted a new warped engine for Smirk's *Endocrine*, and Mr. Smock asked for peace throughout the universe. Ricardo promised to do whatever he could.

Meanwhile, back at the reception, Capt. Smirk initiated the eighth round of glass-tinkling. He and his companion had worked the tradition to new heights of heavy breathing. In a husky whisper, she asked, "Don't you think we should continue this somewhere a little more private?"

"Sounds good to me," Smirk agreed. "You leave first. I'll follow you in a minute. We don't want to be too obvious."

A few minutes later, passersby in the corridor outside Guest Quarters 36-A heard a rhythmic *thump-thump-thump* against the door and speculated that two of their crewmates had succumbed to passion. They were half right; one of their crewmates was succumbing to passion. Inside 36-A, Dacron hit his head on the door again and again, wailing, "Deanna, why Commander Piker? Why not me? Why?" *Thump*. "Why?" *Thump*. "Why?" *Thump*.

In Ten-Foreplay, after everyone ate their fill, Guano mobilized her busboy-aliens. They pulled the ends of the tablecloths around the dirty dishes to form huge knapsacks, flinging them over their shoulders and throwing them into a corner of the kitchen. With the meal out of the way, business picked up at Guano's cash bar. The simpahol flowed freely, pushing many a guest into a pseudo-bender.

The band, Hanky Yankovic and His Polka-Nauts, struck up the first polka. Immediately the dance floor filled with bouncing couples, their stomping oxfords and stabbing high heels creating a minefield for all but the most nimble or those with steel-toed shoes.

One more Midwestern tradition remained to be fulfilled. At Troit's request, the band played "Proud Mary," the song that officially sealed the wedding bond. Mr. Smock took the microphone to sing one verse. His excrutiatingly amateur rendition would have cleared the room if Guano hadn't had the foresight to lock all the fire exits.

Then it was back to the band's excellent polka music. Among the guests were some semi-professional polka junkies, like one pair of nuns circling the floor, facing forward with arms around each others' waists, their expressions grim as they pursued the perfect schottische step. At the other end of the spectrum, little kids and their parents improvised waltzes, the parents riding on the kids' dancing feet.

The music was so infectious that everyone joined in, including many rhythm-impaired guests who realized that with the aid of enough simpahol, anyone could polka.

Capt. Ricardo finished entertaining callers in his Ready Room and rejoined the party. Soon the tea-spiked punch went to his head, and he bravely stepped onto the dance floor for the Hokey Pokey. With uncharacteristic zeal, Ricardo put his whole self in, put his whole self out, put his whole self in and shook it all about. He did the hokey pokey and he turned himself around, which made him so dizzy that he had to sit down for a minute.

Then Hanky Yankovic instructed everyone to clear the floor. Troit and Piker stood in the center while Hanky asked all the single women and girls to come forward. Woksauna Troit knocked down a couple of preteens in her rush to get there first. Others, like Beverage Flusher and Yoohoo, almost had to be dragged onto the floor. They all joined hands—or other appendages, in the case of aliens without hands—and circled the bridal couple while the band played a lively tune.

Piker covered Troit's eyes. When the music stopped, Troit flung her bridal bouquet outward. Despite Woksauna's desperate across-the-floor leap to intercept it, the bouquet bonked Yoohoo on the bridge of the nose, and she reflexively grabbed it and held on. Yoohoo plucked strands of baby's breath out of her eyes and smiled gamely.

As the girls and women left the dance floor, someone brought out a folding chair, and Troit sat on it. Piker kneeled in front of her to capture her garter. The band ground out a strip-tease number as Piker slowly worked his way up her leg. A few bachelors in the crowd egged him on with shouts and wolf whistles. Dacron clasped his hands over his eyes and turned away, murmuring, "I cannot stand to watch any longer."

Piker grinned broadly as he moved up beyond the knee of his bride with still no garter in sight. But his smile drooped as the voluminous folds of Troit's bridal gown interfered with his quest.

Piker ducked his head into the yards of fabric, groping his way through. His shoulders, and then his chest and waist, disappeared into the frothy mountain of white satin. After a minute or so, he popped back out, calling, "I need a searchlight." Someone handed him one of the high-powered instruments usually carried by Away Teams. He dived in again. Several minutes later, he emerged triumphant, holding the garter aloft.

Hanky Yankovic called for all the single men and boys to come onto the floor. They gathered even more reluctantly than the women had, many shuffling out only after Wart walked over and glowered in their faces, cracking his knuckles.

As the band played, the bachelors circled the bridal couple. Troit held her hands over Piker's eyes. When the music stopped, Piker stretched the garter and let go of one end.

The garter sailed straight at Checkout, who was panting heavily from the unaccustomed exertion of walking in a circle. The garter zipped past Checkout's molars and slid straight down his throat. Checkout stared down at his mouth, cross-eyed, and gulped.

"Don't move! I'll help you," called Dr. Flusher. In a moment, she had Checkout flat on his back on the dance floor. From her evening bag, she withdrew a hippospray that knocked him out, and then a laser tool that allowed her to perform an emergency garterectomy.

Before two minutes had passed, Checkout was back on his feet—albeit a little unsteady—with the soggy garter firmly in place on his sleeve where it belonged. He stumbled through the traditional dance with Yoohoo, the holder of the bride's bouquet, stepping on her feet constantly.

Finally it was time to bid the newlyweds farewell. Everyone followed Troit and Piker to Shuttlebay Two and watched them board a shuttlecraft with tin cans and shoes tied to its rear bumper. After their craft cleared the *Endocrine*, Ricardo used the intercom to notify Wart, who had gone to his Tactical post on the Bridge. The Kringle fired a futon torpedo, which exploded just above the cruising shuttlecraft, showering it with rice.

The guests drifted back to Ten-Foreplay. The band resumed, playing mellower tunes now that the evening was winding down.

While his gorgeous companion visited the restroom to touch up her lipstick, Capt. Smirk noticed Dacron moping at a table by himself. Smirk walked over and sat next to him.

"Cheer up, Dacron," Smirk told him. "You know what they say: Women are like streetcars . . . ." Smirk tipped his hand, inviting Dacron to finish the sentence.

Dacron looked puzzled as he tried to follow Smirk's line of thought. ". . . Because they carry many times their weight in freeloaders?" he ventured.

"No," Smirk said. "They're like streetcars because if you miss one, another one will come along any minute."

The corners of Dacron's mouth quivered just a little. "I do not think that is an appropriate philosophy for me," he said. "I have been deeply affected by the loss of Counselor Troit."

"You'll get over it," Smirk told him. "And believe me, you're talking to an expert." Smirk left Dacron sitting there, strolled over to the band, and said something to Hanky Yankovic, who nodded in reply.

As Smirk returned to the table, Hanky Yankovic attempted a Mick Jagger impersonation while his funky polka players lurched through a rendition of Smirk's request, the Rolling Stones' "You Can't Always Get What You Want." Smirk grinned at Dacron and poured himself a glass of simpahol beer from the pitcher on the table.

"You need to get out more, Dacron," he prescribed. "Maybe you ought to come along with my crew when we start filming my new show, 'Wallowing in the Gutter.' "

Guano, taking a break from her bartending duties, sat down at the table with them and put her feet up on a chair. "Whew!" she said. "This is one thirsty crowd."

"What will 'Wallowing in the Gutter' be like, Captain?" Dacron asked.

Guano cut in, "From what I've heard, it's a sleazy tabloid exploitational infomercial."

"Hey, I resent that," Smirk countered. "It is *not* an infomercial." He turned to Dacron and said, "Every week I will *tastefully*"—with a defiant look at Guano—"explore the mating habits of a different alien female."

Capt. Ricardo approached the table. "May I join you?" The other three invited him to sit down.

"Captain," said Dacron, "have you decided on a format for your own show yet?"

"Yes, I have, Dacron," Ricardo said. "We'll take the ship to visit political and academic experts on various planets. The broadcast will engage them in a roundtable discussion of various vital topics, such as political correctness in deep space, the use of Robert's Rules of Order in staff meetings, and the like. I expect some rousing good talks to come of it."

Dacron took a moment to digest this prospect, then turned to Capt. Smirk. "Perhaps I will consider your offer after all," he said.

Now that Troit had left, Ricardo was openly using his favorite teacup. He took a sip, then remarked, "Still, even with the exciting prospects ahead of us, I must admit that I envy the ship that's taking our place in Starfreak."

Dacron asked, "Are you referring to the USS *V-Ger*?"

"Yes," Ricardo said. "Although I've heard that they've renamed the ship. It's now called the *Loiterer*. It seems they discovered that the name 'V-Ger' has been used before." He set down his teacup. "At any rate, those rookies will be conducting official missions all over the galaxy with Starfreak's blessing, just as we used to do."

"Well, I don't envy them," Smirk asserted. "They'll be dealing with Starfreak bureaucracy, and all the rules and restrictions, and the paperwork—they can have it."

"Mmmm," Ricardo reflected. Then he told Smirk, "I doubt that the paths of our two ships will cross from now on. Our personal missions don't seem to have anything in common anymore." He smiled ruefully. "You know, I think I'm actually going to miss tangling with you."

"Ah, but your paths *will* cross again," Guano remarked sagely.

The captains stared at her. Ricardo asked, "Guano, is this one of those time-travel insights you get every so often?"

Guano gazed knowingly at the captains.

Ricardo persisted, "Have you seen something in the future involving myself and Captain Smirk?"

Guano smiled like the cartoon cat that had just swallowed the cartoon canary. "Maybe," she said teasingly.

"I hate it when you do this," Ricardo snapped. "I think you should either tell us exactly what you know about the future, or refrain from bringing it up at all."

"Can't you even give us a hint?" asked Smirk.

"Okay," Guano said. "Just a glimpse. Let's see, how can I put this?" She drummed her fingers on the table for a minute, then told them, "Someday, Captain Ricardo is going to be called upon to rescue Captain Smirk from a terribly destructive phenomenon where past, present and futures converge."

"Oh, no." Smirk shuddered. "You mean I'm going to be audited by the IRS?"

The band wrapped it up for the evening, and an hour later the beer taps ran dry. Still the guests lingered, feeling somehow incomplete.

Smirk and Ricardo put their heads together and came up with a solution. They stepped to the microphone and invited everyone to join hands. All together, with a big dose of nostalgia for *auld lang syne*, or maybe just old anxiety, they recited their creed:

These are the voyages of the starship Endocrine. *Its mission: to cruise around the universe looking for novel predicaments to get into. To search the outskirts of the galaxy for areas with less crowding, lower tax rates, better schools, and classy dames. To boldly go where nobody wanted to go before!*